Jinx's Mate

Alaskan Tigers: Book Six

Marissa Dobson

Published by Sunshine Press
Printed in the United States of America
ISBN-13: 978-1-939978-40-0

Dedication

To my readers who pushed me to give Jinx his own story. For those of you who fell in love with Jinx and wanted him to have his own happy ever after, here it is.

Enjoy this newest adventure to Alaska.

Jinx's Mate: Alaskan Tigers

Contents

Jinx's Mate: Alaskan Tigers

Jinx spent his time divided between his clan, the West Virginia Tigers, and helping the Alaskan Tigers with their journey to unite all the clans. On a mission to eliminate an abusive Alpha, he finds more than he expected.

Summer has lived under the abusive Texas Tiger Alpha all her life. Thanks to her very protective brother she doesn't have the physical scars as others do, but the emotional ones run deep. With a little girl depending on her, she must find a way to put it behind her, and start a new life.

Now on the verge of a whole new world, they must bond together for the sake of themselves and their species.

Jinx's Mate: Alaskan Tigers

Chapter One

He felt the fear that radiated from Manetka Resort, could taste the blood of tortured victims in the stale air. It was once a joyful gathering place for shifters, now a prison for all those who served under the Alpha. And Jinx was there to stop it.

He strolled through the empty lobby to the reception desk, the clicking of his cowboy boots echoing through the open space. The freshly polished wood reflected the light from the chandeliers. Manetka Resort was one of the few places that catered only to shifters. For years it had been a must visit destination. That was until Avery began abusing his members. Now everywhere Jinx looked, it was clear the resort had begun to suffer.

A small seating area sat catty-corner to the reception desk, with large comfortable looking chairs, and floor to ceiling windows overlooking the massive swimming pool and hot tubs.

"Welcome to Manetka Resort! How may I help you?" A girl in her early twenties stood behind the counter, and he could smell the tigress, her apprehension drifting toward him.

"Yes, I'm checking in." He came to stand in front of the counter and set his bag down. "I have a reservation. Jinx."

She glanced at the leather bound book to confirm it, not bothered by the fact he only had one name. It wasn't uncommon for shifters to use just one name. It gave them an identity that didn't tie them to family members. Allowed them to go forth without prejudices. Since shifters tended to have a very long lifeline this made things easier for them to intermingle without centuries-old grudges hanging over their heads.

"It appears to be an open check-out date. Do you have an idea how long you'll be with us?"

"I suspect just through the weekend, but I'd like to leave it open if that's okay. I have some business that I need to attend to while I'm in town, and timing might be an issue for the other party."

She wrote something in the book and nodded. "That won't be a problem. You're welcome to stay as long as you like. I'll have your room key ready in a moment."

"I'm not in a hurry." He glanced around the lobby again. "Slow time of year?" He knew the reason for the place being empty, but wanted to hear the official line Avery had come up with.

The woman paused, and bit her lip before gathering herself. "Actually, we were supposed to have a conference here but they had to cancel. It left most of the resort empty, since we were closed to only their members for the week."

He nodded, amused by the interesting cover story. A conference? Did Avery really think someone was going to swallow that? Shifters didn't hold conferences. Clans had their own things going, but they would never rent out a hotel to hold it in, not when they had their own land to do it on.

"Lucky me, seems like I'll have the place to myself."

"If you prefer isolation, then it's the perfect time for a visit." She laid his room key on the counter. "I've booked you on the eighth floor, you'll have an excellent view of the grounds. No other rooms are occupied on that floor, so you'll have all the privacy you need. Enjoy your stay."

He smiled at her and grabbed the key. "Thank you." Manetka's keys were old fashioned, none of those electronic ones you slid into a card reader. It appeared Avery didn't trust technology. The resort had a website managed by a solitary shifter, deeply hidden so humans couldn't stumble upon it, but that was as far as his technology reached. Even security cameras were absent.

He grabbed his bag and headed to the elevator. Having the floor to himself would allow him to come and go without being seen, giving him the opportunity to check the passages Shadow had discovered on the blueprints that linked the other buildings to the main one.

As he made his way to his suite he kept his sunglasses on, taking in everything without anyone being suspicious. Not that it mattered—the place was deserted. Other than the woman behind the counter, no one else was around. Even with his enhanced shifter hearing he couldn't pick up on any movements behind the walls. Where was everyone?

Stepping off the elevator was like stepping into a ghost town. A thin layer of dust covered the surfaces, all the curtains were drawn, light bulbs had gone out and no one bothered to replace them. The resort was going to need some work to get it back into the condition it had been only weeks before.

Once Tex had escaped the tortures and vowed himself to the Alaskan Tigers, the news spread of what was happening under Avery's control. People cancelled their reservations to the resort, choosing to stay home or go to another resort that catered to their kind, and things fell into disrepair quickly.

He slid the key into the lock, and opened the door. Inside was much the same as the rest of the floor. The only difference was someone had tried to clean up before he checked in. The bedding and towels had been changed, a quick sweep of the duster, but nothing could replace the staleness in the air. The room had been closed for too long.

His cell phone vibrated with a text message. Instead of answering it, he took a wand the clan had developed to check for any listening devices and scanned the room.

He knew it was Ty who wanted an update. With the mission hanging on what he found inside the resort, he couldn't take any chances. Ty didn't like that Jinx was risking himself to do a little recon before they took down Avery. Jinx was the Alpha to the West Virginia clan, and he had people willing to do this for him. It had never been his way. He had Elder guards, all Alphas did, but he rarely used them. He didn't like to ask someone to do something he wasn't willing to do himself.

The scan came up clean and he pulled his cell phone from his belt and dialed Ty's number. Even with another Alpha, Ty couldn't stop himself from trying to protect everyone. Thankful for that, Jinx didn't mind. He knew Ty was just trying to protect him. With the future as it was for the Alaskan Tigers, Tabitha soon to claim her place as queen, Ty needed the support of the West Virginia Tigers.

"It's about time. You were supposed to check in ten minutes ago," Ty bitched.

"Traffic and the receptionist had me delayed." He tugged open the curtains, bringing light into the dark room. "As we expected, the place has fallen. I don't believe there's a guest in the entire resort. They put me on the eighth floor, a corner room near the stairs. Seems slightly odd it wouldn't be closer to the elevator since she mentioned there was no one else here."

"I don't like this. Avery might know who you are, and suspect why you're there."

"I won't be here long enough, and I didn't make it to Alpha without knowing how to protect myself." Jinx slid his hand into his pocket, playing with a silver talisman that had been in his clan for centuries, handed down from Alpha to Alpha. "He's fearful of technology. No security cameras, even the registration isn't done on a computer."

"Tex suspected it, but he was rarely allowed to leave Avery's compound. It was just by luck he was the only one available to go to the landing strip to guard the helicopter until Adam and Robin got there, or we'd still be in the dark about what's happening there."

Jinx set his bag on the edge of the bed and pulled his weapons out. Walking into the resort in full battle gear would have raised alarms, but there was no way he'd leave them behind. "With the place dead, I'm going to scope it out. See if I can find out anything else. In the meantime, call Avery and put the second part of our plan into action. If we can get him away from here to confront him it would be best. There are too many floors, rooms, and passages to take him down without people getting hurt."

"I'll let him know I'm coming to the area to return Tex. I'll see if he's willing to meet me at the same landing strip. If not, we'll have to do it there, so we need you to find an access route to him."

"I have the blueprints, and I'm going to check out the places Shadow marked." Jinx slid a second gun into his shoulder holster before strapping a knife to a wrist sheath.

"Don't get yourself killed," Ty ordered.

"I won't. I'll call you when I get back." He slid his light jacket back into place, hiding his weapons.

"You have one hour or I'm sending a team in after you."

"Make it two. I don't know what I'll find."

"That's the reason. You could end up lying somewhere bleeding out and we wouldn't know it. One hour. If you run into danger get the hell out of there."

"I'm not here to try to get myself killed." Jinx smirked.

"No, you're there because you're an idiot. We don't need you risking yourself when we could storm the place and end it."

"We're wasting time," he reminded Ty.

"Be safe." Ty hung up before Jinx could say he would.

* * *

Finding the basement and access to the tunnels had been no problem at all. The issue came when Jinx realized there were more than just those on the blueprint. Additional passages had been dug out, some of them leading nowhere, others leading to new sections altogether. With each turn he made, the danger level rose. There were too many places someone could attack from. The tunnels were a maze meant to confuse anyone who found themselves where they didn't belong.

He couldn't leave a trail of breadcrumbs, or a rope leading back to where he came from. Instead he counted his steps, marking it down in a small notebook he shoved into his back pocket on his way out the door. It wasn't the best way of keeping track of where he had come from, but there were few options. If he had to run back the way he came, he'd be out of luck.

He could either continue on or turn back. Rather than admit he'd failed, he continued forward. Following the most likely route Shadow mapped, he carefully kept track of how he'd come, the steps and direction of his movements.

His cell phone vibrated and mentally he cursed Ty. This was not the time. According to Shadow's notes there were only another seventy-five feet separating him from what should be the entrance to

Avery's compound. He thought about ignoring it but when it vibrated again he snatched off his belt and read the text message.

Get out! Get to your SUV now! Call when you get there.

Chapter Two

He climbed into his SUV and started it up. It had only been thirty-seven minutes since he'd spoken with Ty, meaning whatever happened since their call had to be serious for him to interrupt.

"Are you somewhere safe?" Ty asked, answering his phone.

"I'm sitting in my damn SUV. What the hell is going on?"

"Drive," Ty ordered before yelling something to someone in the background. "There's an abandoned Mexican restaurant a mile up the road, head there. We're coming to you."

"Ty…"

"We've got to go after Avery now." Doors slammed and tires squealed.

He threw the SUV into drive and pulled out. He knew the restaurant Ty mentioned. It was where they had planned to meet if Avery wouldn't come out of the resort.

"What the hell is going on?"

"He's torturing someone. We can't let this go on any longer."

Growling, Jinx slammed his foot on the break. He couldn't just leave when someone was being hurt. Damn Ty, he'd been right there, he could have stopped it. "I'm going back."

"The hell you are! The rest of your gear is in the back of my SUV. Now meet us there, we'll gear up and storm the place. You go off half-cocked and you'll get yourself killed."

Ty's warning was logical, and without the rest of the gear he didn't stand a chance. Two handguns and a knife wouldn't get him out of there alive, not with over fifty members to back Avery. As it was, they'd already be outnumbered even if Ty and the rest of the Alaskan Tigers that had made the journey to Texas were there to back him. They were counting on the Texas Tigers being so browbeaten by Avery they wouldn't be much contest. Tex also mentioned that no members other than the guards were trained in battle, and there were only nine guards now that Tex was on their side.

Avery and nine guards against Jinx, Ty, Taber, Tad, Milo, and Styx. If anyone could survive this mission, the six of them could. They were some of the best warriors of the clan, while the rest stayed at the compound to protect Tabitha, Bethany, and the others. They had a good chance, but only if Jinx didn't rush in like a tiger in a china shop and alert Avery before the rest were ready.

"Jinx?"

"Damn it. I'll be there." He took his foot off the brake and slammed it down on the gas. "How did you come about this information?"

"When I called Avery I could hear the woman scream in the background. She's being tortured because we haven't returned Tex." The anger heated Ty's voice. "He sent pictures as evidence, with a promise he'd continue through the women of his clan until Tex was returned."

Hearing it was a woman almost had him turning around. Women were cherished, protected, they were not used as torture objects to get someone to return to the clan.

"It was Tex's decision."

"That's not how Avery sees it. To him his members are just extensions of him, property, having no life of their own and no choice." The squeal of tires echoed through the line again before Ty's voice came back. "We're just down the road. Should be there in five minutes if Styx's driving doesn't get us killed first. Where are you?"

"Pulling into the parking lot now." He slammed the SUV into park and got out. "Tell him to hurry up."

"Hurry up? Are you insane? I thought he was going to roll this SUV twice now. If we're wrapped around a telephone pole we'll be no use to her or anyone else under Avery's thumb." Ty ended the call before Jinx could say anything in return.

He stood in the parking lot rolling his shoulders. The anxiety of an upcoming fight had him on edge. Tigers lived for the thrill of the hunt and shifters were no different. Their beasts still wanted the thrill, but this was more than that. He wanted to tear Avery limb from limb for what he was doing. Before arriving in Texas he knew Avery had to be taken down, but now it was personal.

"You don't mess with women!" He snarled. Laying a hand on a woman went against everything in him. It was something he couldn't overlook and wouldn't stand for from anyone in his clan.

Two black SUVs sped into the parking lot, slamming to a stop next to his, and seconds later everyone poured out. They geared up in silence until Jinx's gaze caught Tex slipping on a bullet proof vest.

"What the hell is he doing here? I thought he was going to stay back at the hotel with Robin."

"He asked to come. It's his right to see Avery taken down after everything he's been through. Adam's with Robin, she's safe, that's what matters." Ty handed him an assault rifle.

"Do you think he's ready for it?" It was true Tex had come a long way in his combat skills. Even his personality had begun to return. No longer did he fear his own shadow. But going up against Avery might send him on a rollercoaster ride back to where he'd been.

"Adam believes he's ready physically." Ty glanced to Tex. "Emotionally…we'll see. Robin thinks he can handle it. Actually, she seems to think it would do him good. There's a chance he'll get himself killed but it's his right."

"There's a chance he'll get us all killed," Jinx reminded him.

"I don't think so, or I wouldn't have brought him. He's going to be fine." Ty tied his shoulder length hair back in a leather strap. "Let's go!"

He slipped the rifle over his chest and climbed into the SUV with Ty, Styx taking the wheel again.

"Get us there in one piece," Ty ordered Styx as they pulled out of the lot, heading back to the resort.

Styx sat quietly behind the wheel, the anger pouring off him. Styx was a damn good warrior. He had been an assassin at one time, and some said he killed without feeling. Those who knew him knew it wasn't true. Every kill affected the warrior but he did it to keep his kind safe.

Somehow Ty had managed to surround himself with amazing warriors, those that could be running their own clan but had chosen to serve under him. That in itself was truly remarkable. Just a few months ago, Adam had been offered the position of Alpha over the Ohio clan. Instead of taking it and leaving his position of second to the Captain of Tabitha's guards, he remained in Alaska. The Elder guards were truly an amazing bunch. They'd take on the world if they believed in the cause, even if it meant their deaths.

"Shadow believes this is the direct route from outside to where Avery should be. It's where we're going in." Ty pointed to the yellow highlighted route. "Once inside, Tex should be able to get us where we need to be. He's familiar with the inside, just not outside. Avery rarely allowed him above ground."

"Did it sound like there were others gathered...watching?" Tex asked from the front seat. "He used to like to make us watch when he..."

"All I could hear were her cries, but let's be ready for others to be there. Did he have the whole clan there or just selected ones?" Ty folded the map and set it aside.

"Never everyone, but normally at least a few." Tex rambled on as the resort came into view. "He'll be occupied with what he's doing. He won't even know we arrived as long as we don't alert any of the guards."

"It's possible they are expecting us. He can't think that another Alpha would allow the threats to continue without some consequences." Ty looked to Jinx as the SUV came to a halt.

"Doesn't matter now, this is coming to an end." Jinx climbed out, positioning his assault rifle. Without waiting for anyone, he jogged to the door and swung it open. While his eyes tried to adjust to the darkness he did his best not to gag. The scent of blood assaulted him.

"You should wait for everyone." Styx came up behind him, his weapon at the ready.

"I won't wait any longer while a woman is being tortured. Now if you're ready, let's go." He didn't wait for Styx or anyone else to agree, he just jogged down the hall.

"Turn left," Tex whispered from somewhere within the group. "About halfway down the next tunnel, you'll come to another one on the right. That's where Avery will be, it's the best room to amplify the screams."

The fact that Tex knew this was yet another reminder he had suffered years under Avery. The scars laid witness to the abuse.

Jinx followed the directions, each passageway clear until the last one. A solitary guard stood outside the entryway.

"Take your hand away from your weapon." Jinx raised his gun, letting the man know he was serious.

"Who are you?"

"Don't shoot, it's Ben." Tex stepped closer, moving in between Styx and Jinx. "Ben, don't do anything stupid. Just step aside."

"He'll kill me." Ben's hand twitched toward his gun.

"He won't because we're here to stop him. Either step aside or fight with us. I don't care which but I will no longer stand aside knowing he's hurting people." Tex tried to convince his friend while the others waited.

"How many are in there?" Ty asked.

"Six."

"That's better odds than I thought it would be." Tex nodded. "Now move aside."

"I can't." The young guard shook his head. "He has Summer."

"Then help us and we can try to save her." Jinx moved his gun to the side. He didn't have time to play games with Ben.

"You don't understand, if I allow you in once he's done with the woman he's working on, he'll go after Summer."

Ben tried to explain, which only upset Jinx more. He didn't like Ben's word choice, as if Avery was just working on a car, or working the kinks out of her back, when in fact he was torturing a woman.

"Get the hell out of the way or I'll shoot you. I won't stand here while he hurts anyone." Jinx was itching to squeeze the trigger.

"Summer is his sister," Tex explained. "We'll save her if you get out of the way. Come with us and get her out of there yourself."

Ben stood there undecided until Styx reached forward, snatched the boy's gun away from him, and pushed him aside. "We don't have time for your games."

"Cover me." Jinx pulled the door open, and a flood of screams poured out. A woman lay stretched out on the table, blood everywhere. "Step away from the woman!"

"What the fuck!" Avery glanced to the door, an instrument resembling a scalpel in his hand. "How did you get in here?"

"Through the door." Tex stepped out from behind Jinx, letting Avery see just who had led them there. "Years ago, before you beat the will out of me, I told you that someday someone would stop you. Well, that day has come and I'm one of the people who plan to stop you."

Avery laughed. "Boy, you don't stand a chance."

Tex nodded. "Not alone, but as a whole we do."

"Where did you find them? A bunch of solitary shifters? No Alpha would dare take me on." Avery was cocky and full of himself.

"I don't believe we've had the pleasure of meeting. I'm Jinx, the West Virginia Alpha, and this is Ty, Alpha of the Alaskan Tigers." He tipped his head to Ty, standing next to him. "One Alpha might not, but Ty and I are nothing like the others. We'll fight for what's right, no matter the cost. Now I told you once to step away from the woman."

"What do you think this will accomplish?" Avery lowered the scalpel before shoving it into the woman's chest.

Jinx squeezed the trigger, shooting Avery. It was the first of many shots that rang out.

Jinx's Mate: Alaskan Tigers

Chapter Three

Jinx step forward, his gun still trained on Avery, while his gaze traveled between the woman and Avery. He wanted Avery to suffer for the damage he'd done to the victim, the deep cuts that covered her body, the burn marks that looked like he'd placed an open flame on her skin.

For each mark he wanted Avery to feel it. To know what it was like to be tortured, the fear coursing through him while he begged. It didn't matter to Jinx if Avery begged for death or for his life, in the end death would be the only thing he got.

"Finish it," Ty ordered while he subdued one of the guards. There were no options for Avery, no chance to surrender. He couldn't continue to live because he'd never quit. There were no prisons for shifters.

"You'd kill an unarmed man?" Avery's voice lost the authority it held only moments ago. Now he seemed weak and pitiful, his eyes full of terror.

"She's dead! You've killed my sister." Another woman sobbed over the body on the table. Her blonde hair slipped into the pool of blood as she cradled the woman to her, tears running down her face.

"You brought this upon yourself." Jinx aimed the gun at Avery's head and squeezed the trigger. There was no guilt, not after knowing Avery's final act had taken another's life, that they hadn't arrived in time to save her.

A man came bursting through the door, straight for Jinx. Noticing he held a gun, Jinx launched himself forward, taking the stranger down before he could reach the women. They wrestled across the room, Jinx's grip tight on the man's jacket so he had no chance to get away.

He slammed him into the back wall, bouncing the man's head off the concrete. "What do you want?" Jinx snarled.

"Your life, to revenge my Alpha." The man growled, trying to get a good shot. "I've already killed one of you and I'll do it again."

"Stand down or I'll kill you," Jinx warned. He slammed the man against the wall again, hoping to make his point clear.

"Screw you. I'll revenge my Alpha if it's the last thing I do." He squeezed the trigger but missed his target. The sound was deafening as it amplified through the enclosed space.

Jinx grabbed the gun, and threw it across the room toward an empty corner. "You had a choice." With his weight pressed on the man, he aimed his gun at his heart, and pulled the trigger.

It was over as quickly as it began but there was no satisfaction. Jinx slipped off the body and leaned against the wall. Everything was under control. Tex held back a few of the witnesses, while Styx and Ty dealt with two of the remaining guards who didn't want to surrender. Taber had his hands full another woman, and Tad and Milo were nowhere in sight. Someone had to find them, but first the woman needed him.

"Miss." Jinx slung the rifle over his shoulder, keeping it close if he needed it, and neared the trembling female.

"He killed her." She sobbed, rocking back and forth.

Her pain hung thick in the air, making it hard for him to breathe. "I'm sorry." He laid a hand over her arm and instantly the electricity coursed through them. "Shit." Stumbling back he broke the connection, his stomach turning as he saw the grieving woman in a different light. *His mate.*

The long blonde hair, parts of it red from blood, made him want to run his fingers through it, tangling them in the long strands. Her curvy body made his hands itch to explore. But most of all it was her plump red lips that drew him in, making him want to dip his head and kiss her.

She glared at him, setting her blazing green eyes on him. "This isn't the time. Go away."

"Whoa, lass." He held his hands out in front of her. It was obvious that it wasn't a suitable time to find his mate, but fate never took convenience into consideration. "I'm just trying to help. There's nothing you can do for her now. Come with me, I promise we'll see to her properly."

"He's right, Summer." Ben came toward them, glaring at him. "I'm her brother and I'd like to take her away from this."

"I'm sorry for your loss."

Ben shook his head. "Not mine, only Summer's. Long story."

Ty cleared his throat, gathering everyone's attention. "No one is going anywhere at the moment. In a few minutes we are gathering everyone in the…"

"Manetka's conference room one," Tex interjected. "It will be large enough to host everyone."

"There're some announcements that need to be dealt with before anything gets out of hand. Any members of the Texas Tigers in this room must accompany us there," Ty interjected. "Tex will be leading the way. Please follow him." He turned and nodded to Tex, giving him the go-ahead to gather everyone up.

"I can't leave her." Summer sobbed.

"Ben, if you'll help Tex get everyone to the conference room I'll see to Summer and…"

"Autumn," Ben interrupted, nodding toward the dead woman on the table.

Summer and Autumn; it was too bizarre even for Jinx. He made mental note to find out more about Summer's family, and what possessed her mother to give her daughters such unusual names. Their mother had to be some kind of flower child.

"I'll make sure Autumn receives the proper treatment, and I'll look after Summer," Jinx promised.

Ben leaned in close to her, his hand on her shoulder. "They're going to need my help with the clan members. Are you going to be okay?"

"Go." Her voice was thick with sorrow. "I'm fine."

Somewhat alone with the woman he was supposed to mate with, he let his mind wander. He had always been open to mating, but never expected to find it in a situation like this. If anything, he'd expected to find her once things were calmer. Not in what could be the middle of a shifter war.

Their kind, especially those tightly bound to the Alaskan Tigers, had an uphill battle ahead of them. Tabitha was about to announce herself as Queen of the Tigers, making this more dangerous for them all until they had the rebels under control, not to mention the rogues lurking somewhere out there, waiting for the perfect time to attack.

"Why now?"

"Excuse me?" Jinx wasn't sure he'd heard her correctly.

"Why do you come into my life now? At the worst time of my life I find you. It seems wrong." She glanced up at him, her big green eyes still full of tears. "Mating is supposed to be a happy time, but it's an unsuitable time with the death of my sister."

"Maybe fate threw us together now because you need it." The words sounded too full of emotion for him. He was a man ruled by his head, not his heart. Decisions were made after careful consideration, not by flipping a coin.

"What happens to me now? To the clan? Will you kill us all?"

He reached forward, taking her by the shoulders. Her eyes went wide with fear, and her body trembled under his touch. "I won't hurt you."

She eyed him with suspicion. "What about the others?"

"Let me put it another way, *no one* is here to hurt you. As for what happens to the clan, a new Alpha will have to step up and try to gather the pieces. My clan, as well as Ty's, will be here to help in any way we can." He nodded to Ty, who stood near the door with Styx and Tex.

"We could use you upstairs," Ty called to him.

He nodded, knowing he had to be there in case there was more of an outburst. "Will you come with me? Once it's over, we can see that your sister has a proper burial."

She brushed a strand of Autumn's hair from her face before turning back to him. "Will this pain ever end?"

"No." He took her hand in his. "With time it will lessen, but it will never completely leave you. In time you'll stop thinking about her every second of the day and then something will spark a memory and you'll be right back to this moment. The loss fresh within you, tearing at your soul and breaking your heart."

"Wow, I can see you're a cheerful one. No sugar coating, just *wham bam.* I like that."

"That's good, because I'm not sure I know how to sugar coat anything. I've never had a problem telling people how it is, even if they don't want to hear it. I am truly sorry for your loss." He took her other hand, letting the energy flow through them, warming them both from the inside out.

"Thank you. Autumn was my best friend, my sister. I don't know how to go on without her."

"I know it sounds cheesy, but take it one day at a time. I can't replace her, no one can, but each day I'll be there to help you through it." Behind him, Ty cleared his throat. "Will you accompany me to the conference room?"

She looked down at her bloodstained clothes and nodded. "Yes. My clan members are there and they look to Ben for support. I might be able to help keep them calm. Unless you start shooting into the audience."

"I promise nothing like that is going to happen." Enjoying her touch, he kept his hand in hers and led the way to the door. "We came here to free you from what he was doing, not to kill any of you."

"I hope that's true." She stopped as they neared Ty.

"Come on, lass, he's not going to hurt you." Jinx tugged her hand, forcing her to come with him past Ty. "I understand you're distrustful, but we're not here to harm any of you."

After Ty fell in step behind them, Jinx turned enough to look back. "Did anyone go in search of Tad and Milo? The man that came through the other door said he killed someone."

"Milo and Tad are fine. They were dealing with another group of guards outside the other door, which is how that one got through. He killed someone all right, but it wasn't one of our men. He killed one of his own clan members." Ty shook his head, clearly unable to believe he had mistaken one of his own clan for an enemy.

What kind of training did Avery give his guards? They reacted without knowing who they were shooting at. That would get more people killed than would keep them safe. Whoever took over as Alpha had some serious issues to deal with. The first being security. There were always shifters passing through the resort, and the threat level could be higher than that of a clan with a compound.

Chapter Four

While the newcomers tried to calm the clan members, Summer stood off to the side of the platform with Ben. Her emotions were twisting her up inside. The tigress within her wanted to be with Jinx, standing beside him while he liberated her clan, but the other half of her could only think of losing Autumn.

"Don't listen to them, they killed the guards in the tunnels," someone in the audience hollered.

Unable to stand by as the two sides argued, Summer squared her shoulders and stepped onto the platform. For the Texas Tigers only have thirty members, the room was extremely noisy.

"Hold on!" she called out, determined to quiet them down. "Everyone just hold on for a moment and listen." When people turned and looked toward her, her nerves caused the hairs on the back of her neck to stand on end.

"Say your peace." Jinx nodded, encouraging her.

"Many of you knew Autumn and her visions." Anger and sadness tugged at her heart, making her chest ache. "She believed Tex would bring help when he escaped. He did. For those who said they killed the guards downstairs—I was there. They were given the chance to surrender, but they'd been brainwashed by Avery. This is our chance. Don't throw this away because you're frightened. We're free of Avery, why can't we elect a new Alpha and start over?"

"I elect Tex." Ben stepped onto the platform and stood next to her. "He brought us help and fought to save us. There's no one else I'd rather serve under. Will anyone second me?"

"Second." Mario stood. "Tex saved us. If anyone can lead us, it's him."

"Will you accept, Tex?"

Tex stepped forward. "I accept."

"Then it's carried. I'm at your service, Alpha."

"If anyone would like to leave the clan for solitary living, or to seek a new clan, now is the time to do it." Tex waited, giving anyone a chance to depart. "As my first order of business, I'd like to appoint Ben Evans as my Lieutenant. Do you accept?"

When Ben froze, Summer squeezed his shoulder. "Do it," she whispered.

With a glance in her direction, he said, "I accept." Then he left her side and went to stand next to Tex.

Summer stepped back into the audience and listened as Tex reassured the clan.

"We have a lot of work to do to make this clan what it once was, but if we all work together I know we can do it. You have my sworn oath that *no one* will be tortured or punished for sport while under my command. For anyone caught in the act of harming someone in this way, it will be an immediate death sentence. I will not stand for it."

Sometime during Tex's speech, Jinx moved next to Summer. When he nudged her gently, she glanced up at him. "That took some courage to stand up in front of your clan when they were ready to riot," he said. "It could have forced their attention on you."

"Ben wouldn't have allowed anything to happen. They respect him. He's always tried to keep everyone safe, even at the cost of himself." She frowned, adding, "He has scars on his body because he's looked out for me. I'm lucky to have a brother like him, and I'm so proud of him. He'll make the perfect Lieutenant for the clan."

"He certainly will. I can tell he's a good man. But look—" Jinx brushed up against her as he nodded toward the stage. "Tex has come such a long way."

"He has, and he'll make an excellent Alpha." Summer watched Tex with admiration. "I can see the changes in him like night and day. He cares deeply for the clan."

"We tried to get Avery to surrender so it wouldn't come to this. That's what took so much longer. I checked into the resort this morning hoping to discover the passages so we could sneak in." He glanced around as if making sure they weren't being overheard. "We didn't find out about today's torture until Ty called Avery to tell him we would return Tex to the clan."

"Why are you telling me this?" Summer eyed him with suspicion.

"Because I can feel your questions. You're wondering why we didn't come sooner. Why Autumn had to die." He placed his hand on the small of her back, pulling her closer. "Tell me…how is Autumn your sister but not Ben's?"

"It's confusing. Ben's father is also mine. Our father was mated to Ben's mother, but she had a rough pregnancy and died in childbirth. It's when he found my mother. She was the midwife that delivered Ben."

"That explains part of it. How does Autumn play into it?"

"She was from my mother's first mating. She and Ben fought all the time. She couldn't stand him, said mother always wanted a boy and favored him. I never saw it but they kept their distance. She wanted to leave the clan, to find somewhere away from Ben, but Avery wouldn't let her." She watched her brother as he stood before the clan; this was what he'd been born for. "He's always been my protector—everyone's protector."

"I have a feeling that won't change."

There was an edge to his voice that pulled her gaze away from Ben. Jinx appeared proud, despite the blood and dirt smeared on him from the battle. Everything about him screamed Alpha, which should have sent her running in the opposite direction. The coldness in his gaze when he wasn't looking at her said two things about him: he wouldn't tolerate nonsense from anyone, and he had seen too much death and suffering in his time. When he looked out among the clan, she didn't see pity in his eyes, but sorrow.

"Why do you say that?" she asked.

"When Ben looks at me, I can see he wants to fight for you. To have you mated with someone above him that he'll have no control over worries him. If it were someone in the clan, he could put fear into them so they wouldn't hurt you. With me, he can't do that. That makes him agitated."

"He should be delighted that I'm to be mated to someone in your position. Unless…"

"Yes, lass. Your brother is concerned I'll be like Avery. He's knows nothing else in an Alpha, so it's understandable that he's fearful of what might happen to you, especially once I take you away from here."

"I'm not leaving." This was her home. It might be in shambles at the moment, but it was still her home. She was annoyed he didn't see that. She needed to be there, to help the clan rebuild, to help Ben.

"For us to be together, you must. I'm Alpha of the West Virginia Tigers. Currently I'm dividing my time between there and Alaska. I have no time to divide it between here as well. Mates need to be together."

"You expect me to leave here when they need me the most?" She almost couldn't believe what she was hearing. But why should he be any different? He'd just walked in and started demanding things of her.

"They don't need you, they need Tex and Ben. What would you have me do? Do you want to stay here and have the mating desire claw at you until it drives us both insane with need? Is that what you want? If so, how am I supposed to do my duties to my clan, to assist Ty, free others who are in positions like you were just hours ago?"

The questions flew at her before she could answer them, and each one brought her snarling tiger closer to the surface. She was being irrational, but she didn't like change. Jinx was an unknown to her. When he got her away from Ben and the others, she might find herself under someone's thumb again without Ben to protect her.

"You're scared and it's understandable," Jinx continued. "Even someone who hasn't been through everything you've been through would be, but don't let that stop you from what you're destined to have."

"You make it sound like there's no choice. I'm stuck with you, unless I'm willing to kill myself or you." She couldn't stop herself from smiling. He didn't seem that bad. The body of a god and the heart of a saint. Could she really ask for more?

"I never put anything past a woman." He smirked at her. "There are too many ways for you to try to kill me, not even including Ben."

"Ben?" She whispered low enough not to draw his attention.

"He'd do anything to protect you, including take on an Alpha from another clan even if it meant he'd die. If Ben came after me, even if he killed me, my clan would have the right to demand his life. So before you think about using him, know that either way it will cost him."

"I'm not so heartless that I would risk him. After all, it would destroy me if he died. If I wanted you dead, I'd do it myself."

"Feisty. I like that."

"Not feisty," she snapped, glaring at him. "I simply wouldn't risk him, not when I could do it myself."

"You say you're not feisty, but I can see it in you. You're willing to take me on."

She turned to him, giving him the best hard look she could manage. "I couldn't take you down physically. You'd pulverize me before I had the chance to do any damage."

He cut her off with a shake of the head. "I'd never lay a hand on a woman in violence. Subdue without hurting her if she was a true threat, yes, but never would I raise my hand to her."

Could he be that honorable? "Shifters are always battling over something, and now women are taking part in the battles. One day you might find yourself up against a woman, then what?"

"I told you, I'd subdue. It's how I was raised, and I can't change that even if it means my own death. I couldn't live with myself if I harmed a woman." He reached out and took her hand. "To some it might sound sexist. Someone once accused me of thinking women are lesser beings. That's not the case. I believe women should be cherished, protected. I also believe a woman can do anything she wants. Nothing makes them unequal to men."

For once in her life she was speechless. His words lifted the load on her shoulders and in that moment she realized just how much she had feared him. He seemed nothing like Avery, but in the back of her mind she had doubts. With that simple statement, her worries were washed away.

This man—her mate—was honorable, and she should be proud to be mated to him. She barely knew him, but fate knew what it was doing when the match was made between them. Maybe he was right by suggesting he'd been brought to her now because she needed him.

"Thank you," she said softly. He raised an eyebrow in question, forcing her to explain. "For being you, I guess. For not forcing the mating issue, and letting me wrap my mind around it. You could have said nothing, letting me think you might hurt me. Instead you put my mind at rest. The bond between us is still light because we haven't finalized the mating, but I can taste the truth of your words. It makes this easier."

"I know I can't rush you," he said, gently caressing her fingers. "Not if I want you to accept me."

She squeezed his hand and leaned her head against his shoulder. Maybe things did happen for a reason. The clan was getting a fresh start, and so was she.

Chapter Five

Jinx sank onto one of the plush leather chairs in the conference room. He was beyond exhausted, unsure how he'd managed to keep himself upright for this long. The last thirty-two hours since they'd eliminated Avery had been a whirlwind of excitement, problems, soothing fears, and more that he didn't even want to think about it. Only this meeting with the Elders stood in the way of sleep. That was unless something else came up.

He thought about closing his eyes for a moment while they waited for the newest Alpha, Tex, and his Lieutenant, but he knew it would mean missing the meeting. Instead he leaned forward and poured himself another cup of coffee. Caffeine. That would keep him going for a bit longer.

The door opened and in filed Tex, Ben, Adam, and Robin. Each of them looked as exhausted as Jinx felt. Robin had been meeting with the Texas Tigers, trying to get them to see she was there to help. Tex had ensured the clan that as long as they meant no harm to themselves or others that anything said to Robin would remain confidential just as it would with a psychologist. So far, she'd had little luck in getting them to open up. Most of them were still in shock, but at least she was there to let everyone know she was available when they needed her.

Robin's mate, Adam, had been her shadow since arriving, since no one was really certain who might still be loyal to Avery. "I could sleep for a week." Robin plopped down on the chair across from Jinx with a moan. "At least I've gotten through everyone. Most have nothing to say, everyone seems in shock, but I'll be here when they're ready."

"Thank you, Robin." Tex poured a mug of coffee and stood just to the side of the table. "The guards need a lot of training. Very few of them know how to shoot accurately."

"I'll take whoever you want to the shooting range and teach them how to shoot, as well as gun safety, after I get some sleep," Styx offered.

"I can work with them on hand to hand combat. I'm sure Styx or Taber wouldn't mind giving me help with that as well." Milo took a sip of his coffee.

"I appreciate the assistance." Tex nodded. "I'd never be able to do this all on my own."

"Yes, thank you," Ben agreed.

"We're not just doing it for you, but for them." Jinx leaned forward, setting his coffee aside. "They've been suppressed by Avery for so long that you're going to have a long road ahead of you. But you'll have our support along the way."

"It seems you have an invested interest." Ben cocked his head to the side.

"Summer…yes. You have nothing to worry about, she'll be in safe hands." He didn't feel like reminding Ben this wasn't the time to deal with family issues.

"Across the country," Ben mumbled.

"There or in Alaska, but she can visit as she likes and I'll do my best to accompany her as my schedule allows."

"Your schedule allows?" Ben growled, irritation in his voice.

"Before you get angry with Jinx, I think there's more you should know." Ty stepped forward, coming around to the head of the table. "Being that you were raised in a clan, I'm going to assume you know the legend of the Queen of the Tiger that will one day unite all tigers."

Ben nodded. "Eventually she'll unite all shifters as well, and we can live in harmony with humans. Yes, I know all about that, but what does it have to do with my sister and him?"

"Take a seat and let me finish." Ty waited for Ben to do as he asked. "It's not just a legend. My mate, Tabitha, will be announcing soon that she's claiming her destiny as the Queen of the Tigers. She has the book and the mark to prove she is who she claims." Ty turned his hand over revealing the moon design that had been burned into his skin when he claimed Tabitha.

"It's true." The awe sparkled in Ben's eyes.

Ty nodded. "We have been dealing with things that needed to be done before the announcement. The West Virginia clan has been a great aid when it comes to what we had to do. Jinx has partnered with my clan and will be standing at our side when the announcement is made. As have the Kodiak Bears. So even though Jinx is tied up with this, it doesn't mean Summer will lack for his time or anything, it only means their traveling might be limited over the next few months. Once the announcement is made, anyone resistant to this will see him as a threat as well."

"She'll be in more danger than she was here."

"I will protect her," Jinx said firmly, trying to suppress a yawn. "She'll be doing this to better her kind. Now let's get back to why we're here. We need to know where you and Tex stand. If you're going to be a help or hindrance in Tabitha's mission."

"We're behind you." Tex smiled at Ty. "After all you've done for me, I couldn't turn my back on you."

"With that settled, I'm going to get some sleep. You guys work out the details and let me know what you need help with the most. I'm flexible." Jinx stood, ready to finally get some rest. After all, he and Ty were the only ones who hadn't had a break since this whole thing started.

"Tex, you're going to make an excellent Alpha," Jinx continued. "You have the heart, soul, and most importantly the will to keep this clan together and on the right track. With good people like Ben backing you, you'll be successful and have Manetka Resort better than it was before. Just remember you're in power now. Your authority is something that's needed. Without it, they'll walk all over you."

* * *

Oranges, reds, and pinks danced across the sky as the sun sank low on the horizon, about to disappear from view altogether. Summer stood there under her first sunset in longer then she could remember, feeling the warm breeze on her face, still unable to believe only a day had passed since Avery had controlled her. No longer was she forced to live underground, hidden away from anyone who might have seen her.

Tex had allowed anyone who'd lived in the tunnels to occupy the top floor of the resort. There were only a handful of them, but it was more freedom than they'd had in months, or even years. Avery had kept many of them on a tighter chain, using them to control the clan. She had been one of them, used to keep Ben submissive and under Avery's control. Avery knew Ben would never risk her, no matter the cost to himself, and because of that she had been forced into one of the rooms in the tunnels, locked away from almost everything and everyone. Now things had changed and she was still trying to adjust to this new freedom.

She missed the smell of the outside the most, the crisp air, the roses—everything was so new and fresh. All those months she had missed out on so much, and now she had to make up for lost time. Between helping Ben and the clan, she had spent the day outside, and every moment she wanted to see Jinx. Her gaze scanned the rooms as she walked around the resort, never finding him. He was occupied with smoothing things over. Still, she had hoped he would have sought her out.

"There you are." Ben stalked toward her.

"Everything okay?"

"Things are fine. I wanted to let you know there will be a ceremony for Autumn tomorrow at sunrise. It's early, but I know that was always her favorite time." He placed his hand on her shoulder. "I can't even begin to count how many times I found you two up on the roof as the sun came up."

"How?"

"Jinx and I worked together to get it done. I'm not sure how many clan members will be there, but I know you wanted it. I'm having her cremated. You can decide what you want to do with her ashes. Since you won't be staying here, I didn't make plans for them to be buried in the clan's spot. I thought you might want to take them to West Virginia."

"Oh, Ben." She wrapped her arms around him, pressing her face into his chest, letting her tears fall. It didn't bother her to leave Texas, after all a new start might do her good, but she didn't want to leave him.

"Hey." He tipped her chin up to look at him. "This isn't goodbye. We'll see each other often, I promise."

It felt like goodbye, like her heart was being ripped from her chest. She wasn't sure how long she stood there sobbing, and he held her while she cried. When the sobs finally stopped, she pulled away.

"He's not like Avery," Ben said. "He'll protect you and cherish you."

She looked at him, wondering what brought on the change. "That's a different song than you sang before."

"I had time to talk to him today, and let's just say I approve." He ran his hands down her arms. "He's a good man, but before you finalize the mating make him tell you everything. You need to know what you're getting into."

"Why can't you tell me?"

"I can't, it needs to come from him." He kissed her forehead and walked away.

Ben had left her full of questions. As she sat down on the outdoor sofa, she wondered what Jinx was hiding. She didn't have time to question it when she heard footsteps behind her. For a moment she thought it might be Ben returning.

"I've been looking for you," Jinx's deep voice whispered behind her. "May I join you?"

"Sure, but you missed the best part."

"I believe you're wrong." He sat down next to her.

She turned to find him looking at her, not the sunset. "I was talking about the view."

"So was I." He smiled, and it made her heart flutter. "I've missed you today. I tried to find you earlier but Ben said you were busy."

"I was helping soothe out some fears for him."

"Sounds like my day. I feel like I've been running around putting out small fires." He crossed his legs at the ankles and leaned back.

"You should be resting. You're tired."

"I tried to sleep earlier, but all I could do was think of you. How about you come upstairs with me? Let me hold you in my arms. I promise I don't bite." His lips curled up in a smile. "At least not too much, and only if you enjoy it."

Every nerve in her body sprang to life, firing with need. She wanted to take him upstairs, and run her hands over his body. To see every part of his toned physique that was evident under his tight jeans and white tank top. Her fingers itched to trace the lines of his biceps, and more that was hidden.

"You need sleep, not sex," she said, flushing. "They both start with the same letter but they are completely different."

"I'd like both, but right now I was only talking about sleep. I'm not sure what's on your mind, though." He winked, taking off his cowboy hat, and running his hand over his face. "Things are calming down, at least for the moment. With Ty returning to Alaska in the morning, I need to get some rest. What do you say?"

She bit her lip when she realized she'd misunderstood him. Without giving herself a moment to back out, she nodded.

"Okay."

Chapter Six

In the elevator, Summer considered changing her mind. She hated feeling guilty about what she was doing. Mating was supposed to be a joyful occasion. With everything the clan was going through, she felt as if she shouldn't be happy. She pushed her doubts aside and followed him down the hallway of the eighth floor where Jinx had checked in, and the rest of the Alaskan Tigers and Kodiak Bears had taken up residence, two floors below her room.

"Everything okay?"

"Fine." She answered in a voice that was a little too high pitched for her. When he looked at her instead of opening the door, she added, "The timing is just wrong. I'm burying my sister in the morning, the clan is all shaken up, and here I am about to go into the room of a man I just met, one who came and stirred everything up."

"Would you have rather I hadn't come?"

"No. Just forget it, I'm not making any sense, it's just all confusing."

He slid the key into the lock and pushed open the door. "No, you're making perfect sense. Your feelings are all jumbled. I can sense that, but I can also sense you're longing to be with me. All I'm asking is for you to come inside so I can feel your body pressed against mine." He held the door open, letting her decide.

She threw caution to the wind and stepped in. "Thank you for arranging the service for Autumn."

"You're welcome. Ben played a big part in it as well." He made his way through the living area, and headed straight for the bedroom. Tossing his black cowboy hat on the dresser, he sat down on the bed to take off his boots.

"Speaking of Ben, he mentioned I should ask what I'm getting into. Something about the future. He wouldn't tell me anything, just said I needed to ask you. Hopefully you know what he was rambling about." She stood in the frame of the double doors between the living area and bedroom, not sure what to do with herself.

"I do, and I planned to tell you." He pulled the jeans down his legs, the muscles in his thighs tightening, the outline of his shaft straining against the material of his boxers, forcing her to look away or go to him. She chose to avert her gaze. "Ty's mate, Tabitha, she's going to announce soon that she's the Queen of the Tigers."

"What?" No longer able to keep her gaze anywhere else, she looked back at him.

"You heard me. My clan has dedicated itself to her cause and to protect her. It's the reason I've been dividing myself between Alaska and West Virginia. It's also the reason my brother, Lukas, has taken a place with the Alaskan Tigers. He can do more good for them on their missions than he can in West Virginia right now." He pulled back the covers and slid between the sheets. "Join me?"

"What a moment…" She shook her head trying to clear away the cobwebs. "It's all true, the legend, everything?"

"Yes. It's why Ben wanted me to tell you. When Tabitha makes the announcement I will be there at her back, along with Ty, her guards, and the Kodiak Bears. Tex has also committed himself and the clan to her. Anyone against us will see us as the enemy, and we will be targets." He adjusted the pillows allowing him to lean against them. "As my mate, you'll have your own guards to protect you. I've never bothered with guards myself because my clan is small, but that will have to change. Elder guards will be put into place immediately. I will also be electing a Lieutenant for my clan so that when we're away there's official leadership."

She came to the bed and sat on the edge. "Wow. I can't believe it."

"Does all this make you want to run to the hills as fast as you can?"

"No." She shook her head. "It's amazing. I mean, I never thought I'd live to see the day when the Queen of the Tigers would be here to unite us."

"Not only witnessing it, but a part of it. As my mate, you're very much involved in it. With that comes the danger."

She threw her head back and gave a half-hearted laugh. "I laugh in the face of danger."

"Then come here, lay with me, and we'll face the rest of the danger later." He patted the side of the bed. "Take your jeans off, you'll be more comfortable."

"That sounds like a line." Teasingly, she moved her hands around to the front of her jeans, tracing the button with her finger before undoing them.

When she slid them down her legs, a soft growl rippled from his throat. "I might have just discovered the secret to staying awake. All my tiredness has melted away. Come here."

"Only if you sleep." She pulled back the covers next to him, slipping between the sheets.

"Sleep? How can I sleep with a beautiful half-naked woman next to me? Let me show you how much you mean to me." He closed the distance between them, forcing her to lie back.

"I mean nothing to you."

"You mean everything to me." He kissed the side of her neck, gently gliding his teeth along her skin. "It's so much more than just the bond and desire. The moment I saw you, I felt drawn to you."

She refused to let herself think of the motives that had brought him to her. What mattered was he was there next to her, wanting her. "Show me then." Her own desire laced her voice.

Without giving her a second to think about it, he pounced on her, pushing her gently the rest of the way back onto the bed and pressing his body tight against hers. "You're beautiful." He traced his finger along her jawline, watching her. "I can see it in your eyes that you don't believe it, so let me show you."

With his gaze locked on hers, he slid his hand under her shirt, slowly tugging it up her stomach. "Lay back." When she did as he asked, he teased a hot, wet trail of kisses across her belly, and stroked her thighs with his fingertips.

He slid his hand between her legs, sliding his finger between her wet folds until he found her sweet spot. He teased the bundle of nerves, dragging pleasure from her in hard, hot waves as moans tore from her throat. He held her captive against the bed, his fingers thrusting into her as his thumb continued to wring more pleasure from her core. Fierce desire rose within her like a tidal wave smashing through a dam.

With every touch, she arched her hips to him, demanding more. Her desire soared to new heights, until she couldn't hold back her need for him.

"Please, Jinx." She clawed her nails up his back. "I want you."

In answer, he rose off her, tugging his boxers off.

"Take your shirt off, too," she encouraged.

"So demanding." He tugged off his shirt and tossed it to the floor.

Once he was as naked as she was, he nudged her legs farther apart with his knee, giving him the access he needed, his hand cupping her hips and drawing her closer to his body. She ran her fingers over the hard muscles of his chest before she cupped the side of his cheek.

"Claim me as your mate," she whispered.

He kissed the palm of her hand, and slid into her, filling her completely with his manhood. Slowly at first, with each stroke gaining momentum, their bodies moved in harmony. With each thrust he buried himself deeper and faster, and she rocked her body into him, meeting him with her own need until they fell into a perfect rhythm.

Their bodies rocked back and forth, tension stretching her tighter than a spring as she climbed toward her release. The world exploded around her, and she arched her body into his, her nails digging into his chest, and she screamed his name as her climax arrived. He pumped once more and threw his head back, growls tearing through him as he came. The connection they shared as mates came to life, filling her with warmth as they merged psychically, his emotions and desires overflowing inside her like hot liquid on a cold night.

He stayed on top of her for a moment longer, buried deep within her, keeping the connection alive while she drew lazy strokes down the sides of him with her fingers, feeling the muscles beneath his skin.

"I love you."

The words slipped out before she had time to think about it. They just felt right. He was the person she'd been looking for. Someone to protect her, someone who would love her for who she was in a way only a mate could.

"I love you too, Summer." He slipped out of her and rolled to the side of her, cradling her against him. "There was a time when I never thought I'd find a mate of my own, someone I could share my life with. I had almost given up hope when you showed up."

"More like *you* showed up." She slid her leg over his, getting as close to him as she could. "I thought mates were supposed to feel each other's emotions and desires, but this…this is so much more. There's more then just yours in there. I don't understand it."

"I'm an Alpha. That comes along with the package." He drew his hand through her hair, pushing it away from her face. "You're feeling everyone that's committed to me. My clan."

"Will I always?"

He nodded. "You'll get used to it with time. Once you've met them, your body will begin to categorize them, so you'll understand whose thoughts and emotions are whose. If you need to know something about a specific person, all you'll have to do is think about them and everything will be clear to you. It's helpful to know who is truly loyal to you, and how things stand with each clan member. I know it can be overwhelming at first."

Overwhelming was an understatement. So many different emotions coming at her all at once threw her off balance. She was just a boat bouncing around in a sea of sensations. How did he live with it and not go insane? More importantly, how could she live with it?

"It's all so much. It feels like hundreds."

"Not hundreds. My clan is smaller than this one, but they are a lively bunch. I promise we'll go see them soon. That should help you." He snuggled her closer to him. "It's been too long since I've been home."

She knew it had only been a couple of weeks, but the longing to be among his clan was strong. Many of the members were blood related. It was more of a family clan than she ever knew existed.

"I'd like that, when this is over," she said.

"It's going to be over soon. Tex is already working to turn this clan back to what it should be. The members already trust him because he's one of them. Styx and Milo spent the day working with the men Tex chose for Elder guards. Tomorrow they'll be working with some of the grounds guards. Within a few weeks, this clan will be unlike it's ever been. You have nothing to worry about."

"How can you say that? Tex and Ben were elected, they didn't fight their positions. It puts them in danger. How do we know they won't be killed so someone devoted to Avery can take over?" For the first time she allowed her fears to be spoken aloud. She knew he wouldn't judge her because she was scared for her brother and for Tex.

"As an Alpha, there are never any certainties." He leaned up on his elbow, looking down at her. "Both Ty and I have been working with them. Tex had hand-to-hand combat, gun, and martial arts training before we ever came here. He was being trained as one of the Alaskan Tigers guards. He can protect himself and those under him."

"Ben never had that training."

"I realize that, but he's learning. Actually he's come a long way. He's not going to lie down and die, he'll fight with his last breath. Don't discount him, he's made for this."

With a blink she pushed the tears away. "I'm just scared to lose him like I lost Autumn. I don't want to be alone."

"You'll never be alone. I'll always be by your side."

She wanted him to say she wouldn't lose Ben, but she also knew he wouldn't. Jinx wouldn't give her words just to make her feel better. He told her he wouldn't sugarcoat things, now she had to respect that. Instead of pressing the issue she drew her hand over his chest, just enjoying the moment, trying not to think about losing either of them.

Maybe caring for men of power takes a stronger woman than me. It pained her to think it, but she wasn't sure she was made for it. She pushed the negative thoughts away. If she couldn't have handled it, fate wouldn't have mated her with Jinx. At least she hoped.

Jinx's Mate: Alaskan Tigers

Chapter Seven

There were more in attendance at the funeral than Summer could have hoped. Once it was over, she sat clutching the exquisite urn that held her sister's ashes, her face soaked with tears, and let Ben deal with thanking everyone for coming. She couldn't face the sadness in the eyes of her clan members.

How they had managed to put together such a beautiful service in spite of everything she didn't know. There were so many little details that meant the world to her. One of the only pictures of the three of them was displayed for all to see, and beautiful lilies and roses were scattered throughout the room. The urn even had Autumn's name engraved amidst a beautiful autumn setting, the trees full of color.

There had been so much thought put into the event, including little touches like her favorite flowers, and the urn that made it more special. Autumn and Ben might have never seen eye to eye but this showed he cared more about her than he ever showed. Or maybe Summer just wanted to believe that.

"Everyone's gone." Ben wrapped his arms around her shoulders. "You okay?"

"No." She chuckled through her tears. "I'm not sure if I'll ever be okay again, but somehow I'll find a way through it. What choice do I have?"

"If I could make things better, you know I would."

She nodded, resting her head on his shoulder. "Thank you, for all of this."

"You're welcome."

"Ben…" A voice called from the door. It sounded like Tex, but Summer didn't turn around to see.

"I should go," Ben said, squeezing her close. "Taber is taking Ty back to Alaska today, and we're supposed to have one more training session. I'll stay if you need me."

"No." She shook her head, running her fingers over the urn. "Go ahead. I'm fine. I need a few minutes alone and then I should check on some of the others."

"I'll find you later." He kissed her forehead and stood.

"Honestly, I'm fine." Every part of her hated to lie to him but she wanted him to go. He needed the training, or she might be burying him next.

She closed her eyes, let the silence wrap around her, bringing the memories of Autumn back to her. Grief tore her heart in two, stealing away her breath, until she thought there was nothing left. Anger sprang up on its tail. Anger at Avery, at the clan for not doing something to stop him, at herself for not doing something. It seemed her own life had meant more to her than jumping to Autumn's aid.

Autumn's torture was supposed to be just like all the other times she had to stand by and watch Avery cut away the will to fight from the members. Only this time it was different, costing her sister's life. *She died in order to free us.* At least that's what she tried to tell herself. It wasn't the first death Avery was responsible for, but it was the last.

"May I join you?" Jinx asked, and she opened her eyes to find him standing in front of her.

"Where did you come from?"

"My mother's loins."

His joke brought a smile to her face.

"That's not what I meant. I didn't hear you or even feel you coming." She should have known he was coming to her. It was part of mating to always feel your mate, to know where he was even when they were separated.

"You were occupied." He held out his hand. "Come with me."

"Maybe later, I just want to…" She didn't finish the sentence. To say she wanted to stay with Autumn sounded stupid. Autumn wasn't there, just the ashes from her body, but it was what she wanted.

"I know you want to stay but I have something you need to see. It can't wait."

"What?"

"Ben is about to start practicing with Ty. I want to show you how he's doing. Ty's working with him in the gym. We can see it from one of the offices without disturbing them. You'll be able to see you have nothing to worry about. What do you say, will you come with me?"

She sat the urn aside, her fingers sliding over the smooth surface one last time before nodding. If in a few days she was going to have to leave with Jinx she needed to know Ben would be safe. She had no doubt he would protect those under him, but when it came to hand-to-hand combat he had no training. It was always possible another tiger from a different clan would see this as an opportunity to claim the Alpha position over their clan. The Texas clan was in a difficult position, where it left them prey to others if they couldn't prove their strength.

For the first time in a long time, as she wandered down the halls she saw people moving from one place to another, or gathering together in one of the many lobby areas throughout the resort. It lifted her heart to see so much change in only a few days. If she came back in a month, or three, how different would her clan be? It pained her slightly to know she wouldn't be there to see them evolve.

"We'll come back as often as Tex allows." Jinx tried to reassure her, but it set off more alarm bells.

She hadn't considered the fact that Tex would have to approve their visits. Mating with Jinx had made her the Alpha Female of the West Virginia Tigers. When traveling to another clan, even one that had been her home, she had to have approval from the Alpha. Some Alphas would see her as a threat, especially with Jinx at her side, because of their relationship with the Alaskan Tigers, and soon to be announced Queen of the Tigers. Some might even consider them spies for Tabitha.

"Lass, you worry too much." He slipped his arm around her waist. "Things will be fine, you have my word."

They came to a stop in front of a door with the word *private* etched in bold letters, and he slipped his key into the lock and opened the door. Inside was a spacious office with a large oak desk, and two high backed chairs in front of it. Other than the telephone on the desk, it was spotless.

"This used to be the resort manager's office."

"Before Avery killed him." She remembered that night vividly. Avery blamed him for the low numbers in the resort. He wanted the place full; instead it'd been barely at half capacity.

"Let's not dwell on things we can't change," Jinx advised. "Instead, think about all the members we saved who are now in safe hands under Tex and Ben." After following her in, he shut the door and stepped to the window.

"So many were lost to get us here." Pausing by the desk, she ran her hand over the smooth surface and glanced back at him. "I've been thinking about what Tabitha's going to do, and I can't help but wonder how many more will die before it's complete."

"I guess it depends on what you mean. Do you mean how many innocents, or rogues that attack us?" He came close to her, standing just inches from her, but didn't reach out to touch her. "There's still a group of rogues out there, determined to continue on where Pierce left off. Ty, many others, and myself have been working together to bring them down. We'll find them and eliminate them."

"I understand rogues have to be dealt with. I was thinking of innocents like Autumn, and the others."

His hands glided up her arms, his touch comforting her. "We'll do the best we can to protect everyone. In war, people die. This is no different."

"A shifter war," she whispered, leaning against him.

"In a sense." He held her to him, tight enough to make her wonder if he worried what the future might have in store for them. "Come on, you don't want to miss this."

They crossed the small space to the window. Below, the gym was empty except for Ty, Ben, Tex, and Styx. Wrestling mats were laid out, giving them a softer place to work. Ben stretched, while Ty spoke with the others. Even with her delaying them, they had managed to make it there before anything began.

"Tex is going to work out on the punching bag, while they put Ben through his paces." Jinx flicked the light switch twice, and Ty looked up and nodded.

"How do they know we're here?"

"If you're looking at the window you can see a faint glow of the light. Ty was watching for it so you wouldn't miss anything." He pulled the office chair over. "Have a seat. It will be begin in a moment."

Her butt was barely in the seat when Ty went head on at Ben. Ty yelled something at Ben, rushing him as if he was going to tackle him. Styx circled around him, coming at him from the back.

Ben slammed his elbow into Styx's chest, hard enough that he stumbled back. Ty threw a punch, hitting Ben square in his stomach. A second blow flew at him, only to be stopped mid-strike with a quick block, and Ben returned fire. Quickly advancing on Ty, blow by blow, he forced Ty back.

Styx regained himself and came at Ben, knocking him to the ground. Tumbling, Ben held on to Styx, trying to use his weight to land on top, but Styx didn't allow that. Styx's training was clear as he pinned Ben to the ground.

"Styx is the best warrior. He's been working as one of the Elder guards for the Alaskan Tigers' Lieutenant's mate, Bethany, and is showing just how much of an asset he is for the clan. He spent many years as an assassin, honing his skills because his life depended on them. When he came to the Alaskan Tigers, he wanted a quiet life away from it all."

"Then why's he back in the action now?" She couldn't take her gaze away from the fight, even as Styx stood, giving a hand to Ben. Not giving him time to recover, Ty quickly came at him.

"Shadow, the Captain of Bethany's guards, requested him as her second. He accepted it, and since then he's been taking on more." He laid his hand on her shoulder. "I tell you this because Styx is the best and Ben is holding his own. Mind you they aren't going at it like they would if it was a real attack, but they aren't slacking off either."

"I never doubted he could do it...I'm just scared. He's all I have left."

"Not true, you have me." He rubbed her shoulder.

"As well as your clan." The thought of them put a pinprick in the floodgates she built trying to keep their emotions at bay, giving her a trickle off it.

"You have the Texas Tigers too. No matter what happens between us, do you really think these people will forget what you've been through together, what you've done for them?" He answered for her, shaking his head. "No. You'll always have a home here as well. Even knowing that you were to mate with me, you spent all day yesterday with the members, doing what you could to help them adjust to the changes."

"It wasn't so innocent," she admitted. "I wanted to see if there was going to be a revolt within the ranks. I know these people. I might be able to spot something to let me know they would revolt against the new leadership." She gently placed her hand over his. "Even a small hint could save countless lives and pain."

Chapter Eight

Jinx, Tad, and Milo remained behind in Texas, helping Tex get everything sorted out before their return to Alaska. There was much to do to ensure Tex was safe when they left. Tad and Milo worked endless hours honing the guards' skills, while Jinx helped Tex with his Alpha duties by dealing with the resort side of things, allowing Tex to worry about the clan.

Typing away at the computer, Jinx tried to convert the books into the new system he'd created. It was tedious job, but gave him a better idea of goals for the resort over the coming months. It also allowed him to see just how badly the resort had fallen.

Only months ago the place was busting at the seams, and had a waiting list for cancellations. The resort had activities and luxuries that no other shifter establishment offered, making it favored by many. With time he hoped Tex would bring it back to its former glory.

"There you are." Summer leaned in the doorway.

"I've been here." He leaned back, welcoming the break. "Everything okay?"

"Tex asked me to inform you that someone named Lukas would be arriving within the hour. He's sending a car unless you'd like to pick him up personally."

He glanced at the laptop's clock, cursing when he realized the time. "I guess not, these need to be finished." The pile of papers wouldn't be done by the time Lukas arrived, but he'd do what he could. "Lukas is my brother. He's coming to upgrade things, starting with a computer system. How anyone managed to keep track of the hotel's accounting and reservations is beyond me."

"Avery believed computers allowed people to spy on you. Most of us don't even have cell phones, or any tech gadgets." Pushing the door shut behind her, she wandered in closer to the desk. "I have experience with computers and accounting, from before I was confined to the tunnels. I can do this while you go meet Lukas."

"He'll understand." Slipping a finger into the belt loop of her jeans, he pulled her onto his lap. "I can think of a better way to spend the time."

"How would that be?"

Without answering, he pressed his lips to hers. The sweetness of her lip-gloss urged him on. Slipping his tongue between her lips, he devoured her, tugging her shirt up as he went. Breaking the kiss, he pulled the thin tank top over her head.

"You have work…"

"Don't think, just feel." He kissed along her jawline until he reached the sweet spot just below her ear. Grazing his teeth over the area, he blew his cool breath against her flushed skin. "Work can wait, this can't."

His hand slid around her body, quickly finding the clasp of her bra and unhooking it. The material slid down her arms, revealing her perky breasts, making his shaft strain against the roughness of his jeans. He needed her like he needed his next breath. She was life and could bring a dying soul back from the edge. She was his everything.

Claiming her nipple with his teeth, he gently tugged, making it hard before moving over to the next one. Without breaking contact he reached behind her, gathering the papers and slipping them into a drawer. In one quick motion, he lifted her and tugged her yoga pants down her legs before setting her on the desk.

With a soft moan, she pulled him closer. "I've always wanted to make love on a desk. It makes me feel like a naughty girl."

"Let's check this one off your list and then you can tell me all the other places you've wanted to." He unzipped his jeans, letting them fall down his legs. He didn't have the will power to stop and take off his cowboy boots and clothes. He needed her now.

She stared at him while her hand slid down his chest until she found his shaft. Her fingers wrapped around it and rubbed down the length, painstakingly slow. Her fingernails teasing along it, just enough that he could feel it without causing pain. "I love that look in your eyes, as if I'm all you'll ever need."

"You are." The words were bit off as her hand squeezed tighter, working back up his manhood. He needed her in a way he never needed anyone. "As good as this feels, and damn it does, I want to be inside of you. I want to hear you scream my name as ecstasy engulfs you."

"Take me." She let her hand fall away from him and leaned back.

Without waiting he adjusted his angle, gliding his shaft over her opening, pulling a moan from her. Slowly he glided the length of him in, just a little at first, watching how her eyes glazed over as he worked his way inside her tight passage. Halfway in he stopped and slid out, even as she clung to him trying to force him to stay. Once he was out, he gripped her hips and slammed his length into her, filling her completely. Rocking their bodies back and forth, each thrust gaining momentum.

She leaned back grabbing the edge of the desk, her body arched toward him. With every thrust her breasts bounced with appreciation, calling to him. Without losing his rhythm, he dipped his head and drew his tongue along each nipple, blowing gently on them.

"Jinx," she whispered, her release within reach.

Wanting to watch her face as she came around him, he leaned back taking hold of her hips and sped his pace. Tension had her muscles constricting around him as her orgasm neared, bringing his own ecstasy closer.

Her face came to life with a glow as her world exploded, wood crunching under her grip as his name tore from her lips. It was all he needed to send him over the edge. His balls tightened and he growled as he climaxed.

He stayed buried within her as their breathing returned to normal.

"Oops." She pulled her hand away from the edge of the desk, bringing with her small pieces of wood. Her hand marks had left a permanent feature.

He couldn't help but laugh. Their lovemaking would always be visible on this desk. "A piece of us for the new resort manager."

A knock on the door interrupted him before he could suggest a second round. "One moment," he called out. Then he slipped out of her and pulled up his jeans from around his ankles. "There's a bathroom through there if you want to dress while I deal with him."

Not wanting to greet Tex naked, she gathered her clothes and took her escape.

"Come in." He called as the bathroom door shut.

Tex pushed open the door, a smirk painted on his face. "If you could spare a few minutes, there's something I need your assistance with."

"Sure. What's going on?" He pulled the papers out of the drawer that he'd been trying to get into the computer and looked up at Tex.

"Actually, I was hoping you'd accompany me to speak with a clan member."

"I should get these numbers into the system before Lukas arrives. Can it wait a bit?"

"Go, I'll do that," Summer hollered a second before the bathroom door opened. "Sorry, I wasn't eavesdropping, it's just..."

Tex waved away her apology. "You're the Alpha Female of the West Virginia clan, it's your business too since I'm asking for your mate's help."

Not wanting her to dwell on her new status and what it could mean when visiting other clans, he spoke up. "Are you sure you don't mind dealing with these?"

"No, it's fine." She crossed the space to the desk, and looked at the papers. "Then they're done and Lukas can get started on the systems. Plus, I don't mind...anything I can do. I just hate just sitting around here doing nothing."

He stood, wrapping his arm around her and kissing her. "I'll be back soon."

He strolled from the room with a smile on his face. A quick afternoon lovemaking session was just what he needed to get his old bones moving again. He turned to Tex.

"What's going on?"

"We had a clan member, Cliff, leave. Ben and I weren't sure where his loyalties were. He was Avery's cousin, there was an unhealthy devotion between them. No matter what Avery did, Cliff never went against him. Cliff was brainwashed. I suspected he might have a goal of becoming Alpha." Tex explained, quickly moving down the hall. "He left behind his two daughters with a note saying that a life alone wasn't for them. They needed to stay in the clan, to be raised properly and find their mates."

"Their mother? How old?"

"Their mother was one of the women Avery killed. While I was gone, he killed more then a dozen members in his fits." Tex shook his head.

"You know none of this is your fault."

"I can't help but feel responsible. From everything we gathered, it's clear Avery went off his hinges in those weeks. If I had returned..."

"He'd have killed you." He took hold of Tex's arm and stopped him. "Don't give me this shit, you know he would have and then where would the clan be? You're their Alpha now. It doesn't matter how many people Avery killed, or why, it's your responsibly to put the pieces back. You can't do that if you're feeling sorry for yourself."

"The girls are nineteen and two." Tex continued down the hallway. "It's a large age gap because they were forbidden to have any more children after Ashley. Claire was an accident, which is why Avery demanded the woman's life."

"Wait. If Claire is two, and the mother was killed while you were in Alaska, why did Avery wait so long?"

"He had her sequestered with Claire, away from her husband. It was part of the punishment. Cliff was told if he did everything to please Avery that his mate and child would be returned in two years." Tex clenched his fists. "The two years passed while I was in Alaska. It seems that Cliff demanded his family be returned. That's when Avery demanded the woman's life. Still he kept the child locked away, only allowing one woman to visit."

"Who's the woman?"

"No one knows. Only that Avery allowed her to visit the child, to care for her and play with her." Tex stopped in front of a door. "Damn it, Claire is terrified. She's curled up in a corner crying, refusing to allow anyone near her."

"What do you want me to do?"

"We need to calm Ashley. Then we have to find the woman, if there really is one. She's our only chance to help the child."

Jinx put out an arm, stopping Tex from opening the door. "Summer might be able to help. She can talk to the women and try to find out who it might have been while we're dealing with Ashley."

"There's a phone over there." Tex tipped his head to the side. "Extension thirty-two. Call her and then meet me inside. I've got to help Ben."

The door opened and screaming flooded the hallway. A young girl's sobs mixed in.

What a mess.

Children shouldn't have to suffer for their parents mistakes or grievances with an Alpha. Inside that room, poor Claire was doing just that. Scared, alone, and forced out of the room she had spent her whole life in. Jinx grabbed the phone, dialed the extension, and hoped Summer would answer.

Chapter Nine

With her attention on the stack of papers, Summer was at ease. She enjoyed doing something—it didn't matter what. It made it even better that she was doing something that would improve things for the clan. Even with her leaving she wanted them on the right track, and with each day her confidence of that grew. Each day there were so many changes in the clan, the members, even the resort. She couldn't help but wonder if she would recognize the place when she returned.

The phone on the desk rang, startling her. She watched it light up, the ringing echoing in the room, and debated answering it. Surely it wasn't for her, only Jinx and Tex knew where she was. What if Lukas had arrived and someone thought Jinx was still there?

Timidly, she reached forward and cradled the phone in her hand before bringing it to her ear. "Hello?"

"I was starting to think you wouldn't answer."

His voice teased along her senses, and she could feel him almost as if he was in the room with her. "Jinx? I thought…"

"I am, but we need your help. There was a woman visiting a small child that Avery was keeping in the tunnels, and we need you to find her."

"Claire."

"You know her?"

"Yes." She kicked herself for not thinking of the girl before. "Autumn and I were looking after her. Well, Autumn lately, I was too busy dealing with other things for Avery. Is she..." Fearing the worst, she couldn't bring herself to ask.

"She's alive, but she needs you. Come down the hall toward the reception area. I'll be waiting for you. Hurry." He hung up before she could ask anything else.

Claire. Oh, that sweet child had been through so much, and now she was being thrown into a world she knew nothing about. Her mother was gone, and she barely knew her father. Had Cliff been reunited with his daughter? With her heart breaking for the child, she saved the document she was working and dashed from the room and down the hall.

She found Jinx leaning against the wall, his black cowboy hat hiding his eyes from a distance. She could feel his pain. He was worried about the child. Had he seen her?

"Is Cliff with her?" She asked, coming to a stop in front of him.

"Cliff is gone. He's left the clan and his daughters behind with only a note." He pushed off the wall and took her hand in his. "Claire is in the room behind me, refusing to let anyone near. You're our only hope of calming her down. She needed someone to help her adjust to being outside of the room."

"I'll do whatever I can."

"I just want you prepared. I haven't seen her yet, but Tex said she's in bad shape." He squeezed her hand.

"I'm fine. It's Claire I'm worried about." With a nod, he let her hand go and opened the door.

Inside, Ashley was screaming, her mate standing behind her trying to calm her, but Summer looked beyond them, searching for Claire. There in the corner, Claire was curled up in a ball. The blanket Summer had crocheted was wrapped around her, and her head was buried in her knees as she sobbed.

"Claire…" Summer neared when the little girl didn't look up. "Remember me?"

The little girl let the blanket fall away from her, revealing just what kind of state she was in. Dirt covered her clothes, and her fingers were raw as if she'd tried to dig her way out of the room. She came to Summer's open arms.

"Get away from her!" Ashley screamed in the background. "That's my sister."

"Summer was the woman caring for her. She visited her while she was locked away. Shut up and let her help," Jinx ordered. "Claire's fragile body can't take much more." He stood guard at Summer's back.

"I'll care for her. No one else." Ashley tried to push past Jinx, but he wouldn't let her.

"How can you be expected to do that when Claire is terrified of you? She won't come to anyone. Do you understand what that means? I've seen children give up their will to live without the touch of another. Shifters are more likely, because they need it to survive."

"Ash, he's right. There's nothing you can do for Claire right now. Let Summer help her."

Ashley spun on her mate, anger heating her body and words. "You just don't want to take responsibility for her."

"Think about what this is doing to our own child." Michael ran his hand over her stomach. "We have our own family to care for. If Summer can help Claire, then let her."

"She's my sister." She sobbed.

Tex interrupted them. "She'll always be your sister. Since your father left her in the clan's care and she's a minor, as Alpha I'm responsible for doing what's best for her. Right now, Summer is what's best for her."

"You'd let her take Claire?" Ashley turned to look at Tex. "Even when you know it means she'll go to another clan?"

"If Claire can't open up and trust someone in this clan, what choice do we have? Would you condemn your sister to a life of suffering, solitude, and possibly death just to keep her in Texas?"

Ashley looked at Claire and Summer, sobs making her tremble, and shook her head.

"If it comes to that, Summer will bring Claire back often," Tex reassured Ashley.

Throughout it all, Summer sat there with Claire in her arms unable to believe what she was hearing. She was expected to care for the child. What did she know about being a full-time mother? Nothing. She had been a part of Claire's life since she was born, always spending time with her each day, but taking on the responsibly of motherhood when she'd only just mated might be too much. What about starting her own family?

She pushed all of it away for the moment and focused on the child. "I'll work with her, try to get her to open up. Right now, let me get her fed and cleaned up. She's starving and exhausted."

"Why don't you go back to your room and rest?" Jinx suggested to Ashley. "Summer will call you when Claire wakes, and maybe you can try visiting her then."

Ashley's mate wrapped his arm around her shoulders. "Ash, they're right. This isn't doing any good right now. Come on." With some reluctance on her part, he led her from the room. After the door shut behind them, Summer turned to Tex. "Are you honestly suggesting I become a surrogate mother to her?"

"From the looks of it, you already have." Tex nodded at the girl's grip around Summer's neck.

Ben stepped closer, coming to her other side. "As Tex said before, what choice do we have? Claire needs someone and right now that has to be you."

She looked at Jinx, hoping he'd throw in some logic as to why she couldn't do it. Instead he agreed. "Mate, I believe you've just become a mother. Congratulations."

"How can you take this lightly?"

"What would you like me to do? Rant and rave?" He slipped his hands into the pockets of his jeans. "Lass, you must know that isn't my way. I wouldn't toss Claire out into the world of hungry tigers alone."

She leaned against the arm of the sofa. "This is all too sudden."

"One step at a time." Jinx grabbed the crocheted blanket from the ground and stepped closer. Claire's grip tightened on Summer's neck. "Little lass, I mean you no harm." He tucked the blanket around her. "Let's use my suite. There's enough room that we can add a cot. You can get her cleaned up and I'll see about food."

Ben cleared his throat from where he stood across the room. "*I'll* see about the food. You stay with them until we can get someone else to." When everyone turned to him, he glanced at his sister and added, "I don't think Ashley's going to give up. Claire is the only family she has left, and a pregnant tigress is unruly. I just want you both safe."

"I believe this brings us to another topic." Jinx looked from each of them before his gaze finally settled on Tex. "With your permission, now that our mating is official, I'd like to fly in Elder guards for Summer and Claire."

"With the state of the clan, I believe that would be wise," Tex agreed. "However, I ask that you keep it to four guards. Any more might have some of the clan on edge, more so than they already are."

"Wait a moment, don't I get any say in this?" Summer asked.

"No," Jinx and Ben said without even bothering to look at her.

"See that, Claire?" Summer peeked down at the little girl's dirty face. "That is your first lesson on not giving men power. They'll try to rule you into submission." She smoothed her hand over the girl's back. "Come on, love, let's get you cleaned up while Ben finds you something to eat." She glanced over at her brother. "Ben, do you think you can rustle up some pizza with pepperoni for us? It's her favorite."

"Us?" he teased. "I only offered to get it for the little girl who stole my heart with her tears."

With a roll of her eyes, Summer strolled from the room. Ben was always a ladies' man when there wasn't any danger, and he'd been trying to win Claire over. From the way she moved to look at him, Summer had a feeling it was working.

* * *

Summer sat on the edge of the cot, tucking Claire in. The sleepy little girl clung to a stuffed tiger Ben had bribed her with so he could get the filthy blanket she'd held onto. Looking down at the sweet face, she couldn't understand how Cliff could run off and leave her behind. He had to have known the state she'd be in when they released her from the cell she'd been in since she was born.

"You okay?" Jinx came up behind her and rubbed her shoulders.

"How do you just leave a child behind?"

"Our kind has always done it. Normally it's not until they're older and can take care of themselves. In the states we have adapted to their ways and wait until the child reaches adulthood—eighteen— but in other countries the children are younger. Mind you, none as young as Claire, but some parents don't care. Look at humans, they do it too, and sometimes *worse* things."

Seeking comfort, she reached up, laying her hand over his. "She's so innocent."

"Lass, there's nothing I can say that will make this right or even easier, but you're that little girl's only hope." He squeezed her shoulders gently. "Ashley wants her because she feels it's her duty, but there's no bond there. Claire needs you now more than ever."

"Can I be what she needs? What do I know about raising a child?"

"Every woman has instincts. Trust them, and never think you'll be alone. You won't be. There are plenty of experienced mothers in West Virginia, and Alaska to help you if you need it."

She turned to look at him. "You keep saying me, but this involves you too. I'm not the only one expected to take on the parenting role with Claire. She'll need a father."

"I never meant to imply I wouldn't be there. Claire will be our responsibly if she comes with us. Not only to bring up correctly, but to protect." He pulled her to her feet, his fingers traveling down the length of her arms before going back up. "Fatherhood, well that's a new role for me, one that I'd be excited to take on. I have extensive experience with children, through my clan. We are a very close bunch, and believe strongly that it takes a village, or in this case a clan, to raise a child. No parents are left without help."

"You're serious about this aren't you? We're really going to take Claire with us."

"What would you have us do? Claire is in a fragile state right now. If we abandon her it could be the end for her. When Ashley gives birth, don't you think Claire will be pushed aside?"

She glanced at Claire, sleeping peacefully, and wondered what would happen if she stayed with Ashley. "What about when we have children of our own?"

"You have the bond with her, as if she was your own child. Ashley does not. Ashley is also just a few weeks from giving birth. She's not ready to handle both a new baby and Claire, especially not because she feels it's her duty." He brushed his finger along her jawline, gently turning her head so she was looking at him. "Claire will never be second to you or me, not even if we have a dozen children. I can see the bond connecting you to her. Search your heart and you'll know the right thing to do."

Jinx's Mate: Alaskan Tigers

Chapter Ten

Jinx had barely stepped out of the bedroom when there was a light knock on the door. He had arranged for Tad to guard his new family while he met with Lukas about the upgrades for the resort. He crossed the living area quickly, hoping to reach the door before Tad knocked again and woke up Claire.

He pulled the door open and stepped back. "Come in, Tad, thanks for coming. Summer just got Claire to sleep and will be joining us in a moment."

Tad stepped into the room, glancing around for exits. Every move he made showed he was working. "Milo and Lukas are ten minutes away. Besides this door, is there another one from the bedroom?"

"No, this is the only way in or out except the windows…and since we're on the eighth floor, I doubt there will be any problems in that arena."

Summer paused in the doorway to the bedroom. "Umm…"

"It's okay, lass. This is Tad, he's a member of the Kodiak Bears from Nome, Alaska. His sleuth partnered with Ty, and he agreed to guard you and Claire so I can meet with Lukas."

"We'll be here, there's no need for guards."

"I told you before that I would see to having Elder guards for you. I had planned to wait until we were in West Virginia, but with the state of the clan and Claire becoming our responsibility, it's necessary. I have four guards arriving tonight. Until then, Tad has agreed to stay with you when I cannot." He grabbed a folder from the table and went to her. "Don't fight me on this, lass, you won't win. I need to go. Lukas will be here soon. I'm just downstairs if anything happens."

"What do you think might happen?" She crossed her arms over her chest.

"You were there when Ben said he didn't think Ashley would let this go. There's that and other possibilities, but nothing's going to happen. Tad's here with you for now, and I'll be back shortly. I just want both of you safe. Think of me as an overprotective new mate and instant father." He leaned down and kissed her. "I love you. If you need me, Tad has my cell number. I'm only a few floors away and can be here in a matter of minutes."

"You said that." She smiled at him.

"So I did, but it brought a smile to your face." This time when he kissed her, she returned his kiss with a hunger of her own.

He broke the kiss, forcing himself to the door before they ended up back in the bedroom. "I'll be back soon."

There were a number of things he wanted to see to before Lukas's arrival. Trying to make up for lost time, he jogged down the hall to the elevator. Hopefully things with Lukas would go quickly and he could get back to his family. *His family.* Just the thought of them filled him with joy.

The elevator doors slid open, and Ben was standing there holding a box in his hand. "How's Claire?"

"Sleeping. What's that?" He stepped into the elevator and hit the button for the first floor.

"This is the last box of Avery's demented shit. Can you believe that man kept journals of what he did to us and what he wanted to do?" Ben shook his head, disgusted by the idea. "We're going to have a bonfire and burn everything that was his. Tex thinks it will be a symbol of starting over."

"It will be good for the clan to put it behind them, might help them move on."

"That's what Robin said too. She went home with Ty this morning but offered to come back if we need her." Ben shifted the box to his other arm. "How's my sister handling parenthood?"

"She's just been thrown in the deep end and is trying to doggy paddle. If she starts trusting her instincts and stops overthinking everything, she'll be fine. Any more issues from Ashley or her mate?"

"Not yet. I'm supposed to meet with James in twenty minutes. He said we have a common interest, and we should discuss it. I suspect it's about Claire. I'll let you know what happens." The elevator door opened and Ben stepped out. "You got things covered with Lukas, at least enough to get him started with the computer system and security?"

"I've got it covered. Tex approved the security measures this morning. Lukas is bringing a lot of the computer system with him and the rest will be arriving tomorrow, so it should be up and running the day after at the latest. He'll handle the training for the new system." He followed Ben off the elevator. "He'll be here soon and I need to gather a few things, but you know where I am if anything comes up."

"Same here." Ben nodded and went down the hallway in the opposite direction.

Ben was a good man, and he cared about Summer, which made him even better as far as Jinx was concerned. They had a common goal to see that she was safe and happy. That would make their relationship easier, especially since he was about to take her away from the clan and put her in danger just by being her mate.

"There you are, brother."

He turned to see a younger version of himself. It was uncanny how closely they resembled each other, even with eight years separating them.

"I was about to head up to the lobby to meet you." Jinx gave Lukas a quick hug. "Did you have a good trip?"

"It was fine, hit some turbulence but nothing I couldn't handle. Tex had some clan members standing by to unlock the equipment I brought, so while they were doing that I wanted to see what you had in mind."

"Come into the office, and we'll go over things." He pushed open the door. "There's a lot that has to be done. Computer system, keycards, and security are the biggest. Right now all the guest rooms have actual door keys, which needs to be done away with."

"Coming in I noticed there's no security cameras on this floor. Is that an issue throughout?"

"Yes. The whole place needs wired for cameras. I have Larry coming in with guards." Larry was an electrician by trade, he'd be able to help Lukas with whatever he needed for the new security system.

"Guards?" Lukas took a seat in front of the desk, setting his laptop bag on the chair beside him.

"I've mated, and it looks like I've gained a daughter of sorts."

"I could smell the woman on you but I thought it might have been a clan member. A daughter of sorts?"

He spent the next several minutes explaining how he had managed to become a father to a two-year-old terrified little girl. All the while, his mind wandered upstairs to his new family. He wasn't used to the longing he felt to be near them.

"Wow." Lukas leaned back in the chair. "I never expected you to end up with an instant family, especially now. Are you really going to keep the girl?"

"I don't see any choice. Lukas, once you meet her, you'll see. She worms her way into your heart with her big brown eyes." He slipped his cowboy hat off and tossed it on the desk. "With everything I've seen I've never had the desire to tear someone limb from limb, but

Claire makes me want to do that to Avery and the bastard is already dead. She's gone through so much and all I can think is she doesn't deserve more shit in her life. Stability is what she needs, and Summer and I can provide that."

"Not to mention danger."

It bothered him that Lukas was right, but he couldn't step down from his position or stop assisting the Alaskan Tigers—not with everything that was on the line. Instead he'd have to make them safe.

"I know she'll be in danger. It's part of the reason I have the new guards coming in. Larry, Carson, Jackson, and Garth are the best of the clan, they'll keep my lasses safe."

"Have you chosen a Captain of the Guards?"

Jinx nodded. "Jackson, with Carson as his second."

"They'll protect them, but what about guards for you? With the changes coming, you could use your own."

He had already had the conversation with Ty and Raja before they ventured to Texas. Ty had been forced to make changes in the guards, providing some additional backup guards for when he or Raja traveled. They were going to be in the center of things, especially Ty, since without him and Tabitha having a child the line of tigers couldn't continue. They'd be destined to fade out. It had come to the point that Ty believed Jinx should add a line of protection for himself because of how closely he was tied to the Alaskan Tigers. He had refused until now. Now he was considering it, because he had a family to protect.

Jinx nodded, not convinced he wanted guards. Sometimes what he wanted and what was needed were two different things. "Once I'm finished here I have to return to West Virginia and make some changes. I'll consider adding additional guards for myself as well."

"What kind of changes?"

"That's the other thing I wanted to talk to you about." He leaned back against the chair, watching Lukas carefully. This was something that had been building for some time but he'd always put it off, fearing Lukas's answer. "Due to me dividing my time between Alaska and home, I believe it's time I appointed a Lieutenant for the clan. You're strong enough and have authority within the clan, though I know you've always enjoyed the fieldwork. Would you be interested in returning to our clan and taking the position of Lieutenant?"

Lukas's eyes widened in shock for a moment before he composed himself and leaned forward. "That's an honor."

"That's not an answer."

"I would have to speak with Ty before I made any kind of decision."

He swallowed the lump that was forming. It wasn't an outright no, but it was too close for Jinx. There were others in the clan who could do it, but none that he trusted as much as Lukas.

"I've spoken with Ty. After all, since you're working with the Nerd Crew you are a member of his clan at this time and I didn't want to step on his toes. He said the decision would be yours, and that he realized when you came to Alaska it was most likely temporary because of our clan."

He opened the folder on the desk, ready to put this behind him for now. "I understand you need time to think about it. I only ask that you give me a decision one way or another before I leave here. If you're not interested, then I need to appoint someone else. I don't want the clan to be seen as unprotected or an easy target because I'm in Alaska, or somewhere else helping with the transition."

"It is very sudden. I would appreciate a day to think about it. The clan means everything to me and I don't want anything to happen to the members."

"Very well." He slid his chair closer to the desk. "Let's get down to business."

Chapter Eleven

Summer paced the living area of their suite with a very timid Claire on her hip. The poor child had no idea what was happening but she didn't care for Tad being in her space. The big bear had the girl on the verge of tears just from looking at her, and Summer's nerves weren't much better. In less than twenty minutes she had to deal with Ashley again. She really didn't want to put Claire through it, but Ashley demanded they at least try.

"As soon as Jinx returns I'll leave." Tad sat woefully still across the room, trying his best not to make Claire more anxious. There was a sadness in his eyes that made it clear he didn't like the young girl feeling he was a threat to her.

"It's not you, Tad, it's everyone. She was locked away without anyone around, except her mother, Autumn, and me. Now everyone's gone but me, and she doesn't understand what's happening." She ran her hand down Claire's back, soothing her. "She's going to have to get used to people quickly. Clan life isn't for loners."

"I'm sure a strange-smelling bear doesn't help matters."

When someone knocked at the door, Claire clung tighter to Summer's neck. "Get that, would you?"

Without making any sudden movements, Tad rose slowly and went to the door. "Who is it?" None of the doors had peepholes, so they had to rely on their senses.

"Ben." Tad opened the door and Ben strolled in. "What's wrong with my little cub?"

"She just woke up and came out of the bedroom to find me. Instead she stumbled into Tad. It just scared her, but she's okay." She moved Claire to her other hip. "Right, sweetie?" In answer, the girl buried her face in Summer's shoulder.

Ben stood across the room, not coming any closer. "Jinx is running a little behind bringing Tex up to speed. He asked me to accompany you to the meeting with Ashley and he'll meet us there."

"Okay." She dragged a hand through her hair, pulling the blonde strands away from Claire's grip. "I still think this is a bad idea."

"Me too," Ben said. "Tex and Jinx discussed it. If we do it now, maybe Ashley will lay off and allow you to help Claire. Has she spoken yet?"

"Not a word. If she's not crying, she doesn't make a sound." She glanced down at Claire before looking up at Ben again. "What if she does something to make matters worse for Claire? If she tries to force Claire to come to her, it could…"

"There's nothing to worry about. I'm not going to let anything happen to her. Tad, Jinx, and Tex are going to be there as well."

"Why?"

"Jinx and I are going to be there because we're family, and Tad is your guard until the men from West Virginia arrive. Tex is there as Alpha. If any decisions need to be made, he'll be there to do it."

She shook her head. "That's too many people for Claire."

"We're meeting in the fifth floor lobby. It's open enough that we can stand back so you, Claire, and Ashley can do this without feeling closed in." He looked at his watch. "It's the best you're going to get. Now we should go. Jinx wants us there before Ashley so it will give Claire a chance to feel comfortable with her surroundings."

"Claire." She paused until the girl moved her head away from Summer's shoulder and looked up. "There's someone who wants to see you, so we're going to go downstairs."

Claire shook her head, sending her blonde curls flying.

"It's okay, sweetie. I'm going to be with you the whole time. To get there, we're going to take an elevator with Tad and Ben. I promise you're going to be fine, they're here to protect us." She tried to soothe the girl, but she wasn't sure if she was making things better or worse.

Her doubts began to rise within her. She knew nothing about raising a child. Not to mention the fact Claire had yet to speak. How was she supposed to deal with that? Claire had always been a quiet child, but this was more than that. She was completely silent.

* * *

Jinx stood in the back of room watching his mate work her magic on little Claire. In just the few minutes he had been watching, Summer had gotten Claire to sit on her lap without burying her head away. The little cub wouldn't look at Tad, but she clung to the stuffed tiger Ben had brought her earlier. Summer had doubts about being an instant parent to Claire, but already she was proving she was the only one capable of the job. Claire trusted her, and with half the tiger shifter cubs not making it past their second birthday, they need Summer and Claire to keep the bond strong.

Claire might already be two but she wasn't out of the woods yet. There was still a high casualty rate until cubs reached five. Three more years that Claire would be relying on Summer and Jinx for everything—they were her key to survive in a clan. Maybe longer due to what she'd suffered already. Either way, they'd be there for her.

"Look what I have for the little lass." Jinx came toward them carrying the crocheted blanket.

With a bright smile, the first one Jinx had seen since he met her, Claire held out her hand for the blanket. She didn't say anything, but this was a start.

"Have you seen Ashley?" Summer whispered as he neared.

"Tex headed them off, giving me time to slip up here to make sure things were okay. They'll be up in a few minutes. Is she ready?"

"As ready as she's going to be." She draped the blanket over Claire's legs. "As long as Tad keeps his distance she's okay. For some reason he scares her."

"Ben and I both brought her gifts, maybe Tad just needs to bribe her." He knelt down so he was at eye level with Claire. "Mind if I sit next to you two beautiful lasses?" Instead of answering, she pulled the blanket closer to her face, snuggling with it and the tiger. He took that as a yes, and sat next to them.

"Things are going to be fine, Summer?" Several feet away, Ben stood off to the side.

"I hope so. If things go badly, it could be disastrous for Claire." The elevator dinged and she hugged the girl to her.

"Let the show begin," Ben whispered.

"For Claire's sake, I hope it won't be a show." Jinx slid his arm around Summer's back.

Ashley strolled in—maybe *waddle* was a better word—with her hand on her stomach. She was due any day and it showed. Her belly was round and full with the cub she carried. Her eyes were still red and puffy from crying. Her mate, Michael, walked behind her.

"Claire!" She cried out, holding her arms open as if she expected the girl to run to her. When she didn't, Ashley glared at Summer. "You've turned her against me."

"How could she have done that?" Tex asked, coming farther into the lobby sitting room.

"I don't know, but she did. I'm her sister."

Claire cuddled deeper against Summer, holding tighter. "She doesn't know you as family," Summer said calmly. "She's scared, and you coming in here screaming isn't helping anything. How about you sit down and we do this at Claire's pace? You can't expect miracles."

"Who do you think you are giving me orders?" Ashley raved until her mate placed a hand on her shoulder.

"Ash…" Michael began until Ashley turned and glared at him.

"Summer's right. Sit down or you can leave," Tex ordered. "I won't have you doing more harm to the child."

"You would force me from her life? I thought this clan you're building was supposed to be about family, and responsibilities. Or does that only apply when it suits you?"

"Ashley, you are out of line." Michael took hold of her arm.

"No, he's out of line trying to keep me away from her." She gripped her stomach as a cry of pain tore through her lips.

"Are you okay? Do we need to get a doctor?" Michael wrapped his arm around her, keeping her on her feet. "See what you're doing to yourself and our child?"

"No doctor." She cried out, pain lacing her words.

"Let her sit." Ben pushed a chair over so Ashley didn't have to move. When she sat, he knelt next to her. "Look at Claire. Really look at her, and see what this is doing to her. Is this what you want her to remember?"

"She'll remember I fought for her."

"No, she'll remember the fighting, the anger. She's scared and you're making it worse." He held up a hand before she could cut him off. "I know you're family, but she doesn't know you. Blood means little when you're scared. Right now all she knows is her mother is gone, and Summer is the only one who's familiar to her."

"What do you want me to do?"

"You can see Summer cares for the girl. Why not let her help Claire adjust to this new life? She's been through a lot, and forcing her to stay with you when she's terrified is only going to make matters worse." Ben glanced back to Summer and Claire. "You know she'll be leaving once Jinx has helped with the security issues for the resort, but they'll be back often so you can see Claire. If things change in the future, we can reevaluate it then."

"Claire needs help." Jinx waited until Ashley looked at him. "She hasn't spoken to anyone, not even Summer, since she was brought out of her prison. You met Robin, the therapist from the Alaskan Tigers clan. She believes Summer can help."

"You swear she'll help her?" There was a pity in Ashley's voice that wasn't there before.

"We'll do everything we can for her." Summer soothed the last of the tension from the little girl's shoulders. "I didn't realize it before, but every day I'd go visit Claire, she won my heart. I love her as if she was my own flesh and blood. I'll do right by her."

"What about you?" Ashley glared at Jinx. "Are you going to be jealous of having to share your new mate with Claire? Will she be forced aside so you can have Summer to yourself? Or once Summer is pregnant with your own child?" Ashley shot the questions at Jinx faster than he could answer.

"Summer will be like a daughter to both of us. She'll want for nothing, not love, attention, or material things. She'll be surrounded by people who love and care for her in West Virginia, as well as here."

Ashley looked to Tex who stood silently waiting. "You swear you'll let them come back?"

Tex nodded. "They are no threat to this clan, and are always welcome. We will forever be indebted to Jinx's clan as well as the Alaskan Tigers for what they've done for us."

"Then take her." Ashley stood and rushed out of the room.

"I have to go after her." Michael glanced around the room before settling on Ben. "You better be right on this. If not, she'll never forgive any of us."

Jinx watched him go after Ashley. "What did he mean by that?"

"Michael and I met earlier." Ben took the seat Ashley had vacated. "He worked on her even before she came here."

"You forced them to see our way?" Summer's voice held an edge of anger.

"No, only to see what was right for Claire. If I thought Ashley could have handled the care she needs, and the new baby, I would have fought for them. You know Ashley, she can't handle it, even Michael didn't believe she could. It isn't about you being my sister, it's about what's right for Claire."

Jinx was slightly amazed that Ben was able to overlook the bond he had with Summer and think only of the child. It proved that Tex had chosen right when he picked his Lieutenant. The Texas Tigers were on their way to a very happy future.

Chapter Twelve

With Claire asleep, Summer collapsed on the sofa, emotionally exhausted. The day had been trying and it wasn't over yet. Ben and Jinx had brought her belongings and piled them up in the middle of the living area for her to go through and decide what she wanted to take with her. There were also six or more bags of things that another mother with a daughter Claire's age had sent over. It saved them from having to rush out and shop since Claire had very little when it came to clothes and toys.

"Here's the last of the stuff." Ben entered, his arms full of more bags.

She lifted her head enough to see him pile it on top of everything else. "What is all that?"

"Ashley said if she couldn't keep Claire, she wanted to get her everything she needed to start her new life. There's clothes, toys, shoes, and my favorite." He reached into the largest bag and pulled out a stuffed Dalmatian that had to be as big as Claire. "Spot."

"Oh, that's cute." She scooted up on the sofa. "It will be nice that she won't have to keep anything from downstairs."

"Anything but that blanket we can't pry away from her," Jinx reminded her.

She gently kicked her mate who was sitting rubbing her feet. "That's your fault. You gave it back to her, she was perfectly content with the stuffed tiger."

"I only wanted to make her feel safe, and the way she held onto that dirty blanket before, I thought it would help. At least it's clean now, and it did help, so you can thank me later." Jinx winked at her.

"We'll see about it. I might be too tired once I get through all that stuff. Plus if you haven't forgotten, we have a two-year-old child sleeping next to the bed. That doesn't exactly turn me on."

"There's always the shower." He tickled her instep, making her squirm. "How about we just throw it all onto the plane and then you don't have to worry about it?"

"Then I'll have to worry about it in West Virginia. No use lugging what we don't want anywhere else. Plus you're supposed to be meeting with Lukas again, and your men will be flying in soon." She hated to remind him since that meant he'd leave her alone with Tad or someone else when all she wanted to do was cuddle next to him.

"I asked Lukas to meet me here so I wouldn't have to leave you. The guards will also stop by, then they'll take their rooms across the hall. No guards on duty tonight, unless I'm called away. They can rest and I can have you all to myself while Claire sleeps."

"That sounds like heaven." She pulled her feet away and cuddled into his chest.

"You two are sickening." Ben teased.

"You're just jealous. You want a mate of your own," she told him. "Are you sticking around?"

"No, we're having the bonfire tonight." He tossed the Dalmatian onto the stack. "If you need anything just holler, otherwise I'll see you in the morning."

When the door closed behind Ben, Jinx nuzzled her neck. "Umm, to be alone with you finally."

"Not actually alone," she reminded him. Gosh, she couldn't wait until they weren't sharing the room with Claire, and she could have her way with him again. "We're doing the right thing for her, aren't we?"

He stopped what he was doing and looked at her. "Yes. You're what's right for her."

"But taking her away…"

"Away from what? She doesn't know this place or anyone here. Now is the best time to get her away, let her start fresh somewhere else. Which is why as long as Lukas keeps things on track, we are flying out the day after tomorrow."

Her heart skipped a beat with the thought of going to West Virginia. In the mix of everything she had forgotten she still had to meet his clan. What if they didn't accept her? Or worse, what if they didn't accept Claire?

"I see my little worrier is back." He teased. "Everything is going to be fine. They'll love you, just as I do. Word is already spreading around the clan. Everyone is excited I'm bringing a mate and child home. It's a big deal when the Alpha finds his mate. It brings new life into the clan, and the clan's population increases with new births."

"What about Lukas? Has he made a decision about your offer?"

"Not yet." He frowned at her. "I told you before I didn't hold high hopes for it. He enjoys his work with Connor, the Nerd Crew, and being in the field. If he took the position of Lieutenant he'd be out of the field for the most part. If work with Connor could be done remotely, it might sway him, but I'm not sure any of that's the same for him."

"He'll come around."

"If he passes on this chance it might be too late. He's one I'd trust at my back, to keep you, Claire, and the clan safe if anything happened to me." A knock at the door stopped him for a moment. "There he is."

She stopped him as he tried to get up. "Nothing's going to happen to you. Things are going to work out with the Lieutenant position. Just like they worked out for my clan, and for Claire."

* * *

Jinx planted a smile on his face and pulled open the door. He didn't want Lukas to know he was worried if the Lieutenant position would be filled or not. Lukas still had roughly forty-eight hours before Jinx was leaving for West Virginia.

"Hey brother, you better be bringing me good news."

"A little of both." Lukas stepped into the suite, his arms loaded with paperwork and his laptop. "Ahh, you must be the woman who finally got Jinx to settle down."

"Summer." She held out her hand to him.

"I'm Lukas. The more handsome one if I do say so myself." Lukas took her hand and kissed it.

"Quit flirting with my mate," Jinx ordered. "Sit down and tell me this news."

"Duty calls," Summer said, before going to the pile of things she needed to go through.

"Frequently, when Jinx is in charge." Lukas placed his things on the coffee table and sat down. "Mating hasn't changed you one bit, you're still all business. Where's the play, old man?"

"There's a time for play and a time for work. Don't call me old man." Jinx grabbed the can of soda he had abandoned earlier and took a swig. "So on with it."

"Very well. I have things in place for Larry to start with the cameras tomorrow morning. All the spots are marked, and once in place the whole resort will be covered. Tex has also requested some of the outside and clan areas be covered under a different monitoring system, which I'll begin working on tomorrow." Lukas handed him papers with all the camera locations listed.

"How about the resort computer system? Keyless entry cards for the doors?"

"The computer system should be up and running tomorrow night. I'm just waiting on a few pieces to arrive, which are due here by tomorrow noon. The keyless entries, well…"

"What?" Jinx pressed.

"All the doors will need to be replaced, and the new ones will take a week from the manufacturer. That's going to push it back. In the meantime the clan can start getting other things in place, cleaning the rooms, painting, everything else. That way, when the new doors are in place they can reopen the resort."

"Has Tex decided who will head up security?"

"Ben's going to be in charge. He's very good with computers. There will also be a guy named Barry handling the day-to-day security details. I've already brought Ben up to date with everything." Lukas pushed the papers aside and powered the computer up.

"I won't be here to oversee everything, but I can leave Larry behind to help." Jinx looked over the papers.

"Look at this." Lukas turned the laptop. "Here's a three-dimensional diagram of the resort. The red circles are where the cameras are going. The top floor will be Tex and Ben's private quarters. They are also keeping one there for you and Summer when you visit. The next floor will be quarters for any workers or single members who wish to remain in the building. The rest of the clan will take up residence in the other building around back. It's more suited for families with more apartment living, and there are also some stand alone homes."

"Seems like they have everything worked out."

"That's sweet of them to keep a place for us." Summer moved a pile of stuff aside.

"According to them, there will always be a place for you here." He clicked a few buttons and the screen changed. "These will be the changes once everything is complete. A total renovation, giving the resort a new image to show the new Alpha."

"Whose idea was that?" Jinx looked over the design. It was perfect, a clear way to say it was under new management, and would get people to return to check out the changes.

"Tex. He sketched out what he wanted for the logo, design, and ideas for the rooms. I put it together. There's a team ready to start right way, the sign and other supplies should be here soon."

"Everything is coming together. It's all going to work out for them." Summer leaned over Jinx's shoulder. "I'm sorry. I shouldn't interrupt you."

"You're fine, lass." He laid his hand over hers. "It's nice to see, isn't it?"

"Yes." She nodded. "To know the clan will be fine once we leave…that means a lot to me."

"They'll have weeks before things are complete but when it's done it will be like a new gem. Everyone will be coming to see it." Lukas's eyes sparkled as he spoke. "I've added some other touches, mostly with activities and things that I believe the clientele will enjoy. Tex is considering them as we speak. In the meantime I'm going to work on a new website for them, which I'll maintain, instead of outsourcing it."

"You're going to be busy with all of this." Jinx had to swallow his disappointment; his brother would have no time to accept the offered position.

"It won't take much time, plus I'll have weeks before the website needs to be complete. Actually I wanted to…"

Jinx's phone began ringing, interrupting their conversation.

"One second." Jinx grabbed his cell phone off the table and brought it to his ear. "Yes?"

"Boss, we've just pulled up out front. Where would you like us to meet you?" Jackson's husky voice came through the line.

"Just wait there, I'll be down in a moment." He slid his finger over the screen, ending the call before turning to Lukas. "Could you stay with Summer and Claire for a few minutes while I go meet Jackson and the guys and show them to their rooms?"

"No problem. Take as long as you need." Lukas nodded. "I'll leave copies of all this for you on the coffee table."

Jinx rose, slipping his arm around Summer's waist. "I'll be back in just a few minutes. Jackson might be coming back with me to meet you and go over a few things, depending on how tired he is."

"I'll be here." She kissed him. "There's a lot more I need to go through, so take your time."

Chapter Thirteen

Clothes and toys were stacked in piles of what was going and what wasn't. The stack they would bring with them was getting fuller than she expected. Two empty suitcases sat off to the side, but with the height of the pile she was doubtful there would be enough room.

"Penny for your thoughts?" she asked Lukas, who sat on the sofa, the laptop in front of him. But he wasn't working, instead he was gazing into space.

"I'm thinking about West Virginia, my home." He sat the computer aside and looked at her. "I never expected to leave the clan, but when I got the chance to stay in Alaska to help with their cause I jumped at it. For the first time I felt like I was needed, that I was doing something good."

"What changed?"

"Jinx…" He let his head fall back against the sofa. "This opportunity…well, it's got me thinking. I miss home, and it's a once in a lifetime chance. If I turn it down, I might never be offered the chance again."

"But?" She provoked him when he went silent.

"I've grown a lot since I've left West Virginia. I'm not sure I'm willing to give everything up. I still want to have a part in all the changes. At the same time, my duty lies with the family clan. I feel so split."

"Have you talked to Jinx about this? Maybe there's a way to do both. He's very committed to the changes, and the Alaskan Tigers. I don't see why it wouldn't work for you. You could continue working with them, maybe remotely?"

"I was going to mention it, but then Jackson called." He glanced over at her, giving her a halfhearted smile. "I shouldn't be bothering you with my problems when you have your own."

"It's fine. What else are families for?" She tossed the Dalmatian into the keep pile. "How about a cup of coffee?"

"Sure. It might help clear my mind. I'll get it." He stood and went to the small kitchenette.

"I know Jinx is hopeful that you will take the position, but in the end you have to do what's right for you. If the two of you can work out something so you're both happy then all the better." She got up from the floor, stepping over the piles she'd created. "He cares about your happiness, and he'll understand, no matter what you decide."

"What about you? You're Alpha Female of the clan. Did he give you any say in it?"

"He mentioned it to me before he asked you, but as for anything further…no. We didn't discuss any others he might have in mind if you decline the position. Not that I could have been much help since

I've never met any of the clan members." She took the coffee mug he offered and sat down at the table that was now clear since everything was in piles on the floor. "I'm aware he does have another in mind because he doesn't feel you'll take the position. I also know he doesn't have the same faith in the other person as he does you. He believes you'll keep the clan safe if something happens to him."

"That's the other thing…" He brought his own coffee over and sat down next to her. "Heaven forbid something happened to Jinx. I don't think I could stand by and see the clan fall into someone else's hands. But since I'm not even a clan member I wouldn't have the right to challenge whoever took over. When the Lieutenant is forced to take over the clan, only a current clan member can challenge him."

"I've heard of outsiders challenging before."

"True, but it's not the way of our kind. Most times they are desperate to lead, and the clan will overthrow them within weeks. A clan normally won't stand for an outsider coming in to overthrow their new Alpha without them at least giving the new Alpha a chance or challenging him themselves."

She sat there listening to him and felt like an outsider. These were her people they were talking about, and she barely knew anything about them. Avery had brainwashed the clan, making them believe they were stuck under him and that no one could overthrow him. Ben had tried to get people to see that if they rallied together they could defeat Avery but everyone was too far-gone to listen to him. They wouldn't risk Avery's wrath on a chance. Instead they'd rather hide in the shadows hoping they wouldn't catch his attention.

"You might not like to hear this, but I'm going to say it anyway." She leaned forward, placing her hand over his. "If you don't want to see someone else possibly running the clan, then you need to take the position."

"I love that you make it sound so easy."

She nodded, and picked up her mug. "It can be if you want it to be."

Jinx opened the door before she could add anything more.

Behind him was a tall man with the greenest eyes she'd ever seen, his hair cut in military style. His muscles strained against his flannel shirt and tight jeans. Just by looking at him she knew he didn't get them from hours in the gym; everything about him screamed he was an outdoorsman. Any workout he did was in the fresh air.

"Summer, this is Jackson, the Captain of your Guards." He glanced behind him and tipped his head in her direction. "Jackson, my mate."

Jackson came to her, dropping to his knees in front of here, and took her hand in his. "I'm in your service now and always."

She glanced at Jinx. The realization of what he was doing was overwhelming.

"Do you know what to do?" Jinx asked.

"I've seen others do this in front of Avery, but I never expected…"

"You are my mate, the clan's Alpha Female." He let his gaze shift between her and Jackson who was still kneeling in front of her. "He is offering you his neck. When a lesser shifter comes into the presence of their Alpha, or Alpha Female, for the first time, they are supposed to offer you their neck. You then bend and sniff it. This act shows they are subservient to you, and that you accept them as part of your clan. This marks your scent on them as well, so another Alpha or rogue knows they are messing with a clan, not a lone shifter."

Summer felt her heart speed up with the thought that the clan was hers as well, not just Jinx's. She'd have people depending on her, duties to the clan. Now she completely understood what Lukas was going through.

"Jackson, I didn't consider how much rule Avery had over his people, I should have prepared her," Jinx explained as she delayed.

She leaned forward and sniffed Jackson's neck. The scent of crisp fall leaves, cedar and maple trees, mixed with the clean smell of air after a rainstorm filled her. It was strong enough that she almost believed she was there, with the wet dirt under her feet, surrounded by woods. She longed to be there, to be…*home*. For the first time in her life, she felt as if she actually belonged somewhere.

Not wanting the feeling to end, she took another deep breath of it, and everything clicked into place. Jackson's emotions slipped into a file, all nice, neat, and together. No longer was he lost in the jumble that was the rest of the clans.

While her eyes were closed, Jinx came to her and placed his hand on her shoulder, as if he was trying to ground her. "You're smelling the clan. It's heavenly, I know, but don't lose yourself to it. We'll be there soon and everything else will come together." He squeezed her shoulder, pulling her back from the edge of bliss. "If you mean Jackson no harm, kiss his neck and welcome him to the clan. If you find him a threat or wish him harm, this is your chance to bite his neck, at least until you draw blood, depending on the situation and the punishment you see fit."

She knew with everything in her that he meant no harm to her, Jinx, or Claire. He'd protect them with his dying breath. She leaned in, allowing her lips to touch his neck, and placed a soft kiss there.

"You have now accepted Jackson as subservient to you. This is how the pack greets the Elders when they have been away for a while or they're receiving judgment over a crime."

Jackson stood. "It's an honor to serve under you."

"Thank you." She shot a look behind her to Jinx. "Not that I need guards."

"Let's not do that again." He rubbed her shoulder. "I want you and Claire protected."

"Very well. Jackson, I'm sorry about the mess, but feel free to make yourself at home. If you'll excuse me I'm going to take a hot bath." She rose and kissed her mate before heading to the adjourning bedroom. On the way, she shot Lukas a look and mouthed, *Talk to him.*

* * *

Jinx fought everything in him not to go after her. Knowing she was in the next room, getting naked and stepping into a steaming hot bubble bath, made his shaft harden. Instead, he forced himself to clean off another chair and deal with the security detail.

"Have a seat, Jackson." He nodded to the empty chair before seating himself. "Lukas, I'd like to continue with what we started after I go over a few quick things with Jackson, unless you have somewhere you need to be."

"No, I'm done for the night. While you do that, I'll just mosey over there and work on my computer."

"Very well." Jinx turned back to Jackson. "I'll cut straight to the point because I know you're tired. I asked you to be the Captain of Summer's guards because I know you can protect her. The safety of her and Claire is the most important."

Over the next few minutes, he brought Jackson up to speed. He went into the details of Tabitha's coming announcement as Queen of the Tigers, to why he had been spending so much time in Alaska, to how Claire had come to be his adopted daughter. Everything that was relevant to keeping his family safe was on the table for Jackson to absorb.

"I know this is a lot to take in," he added, "but you need to know everything in order to keep her safe."

"I understand, and even with the challenges ahead I'll do what you ask." Jackson clasped his hands on the table. "However, I have to suggest that we add more guards to their protection."

"We will, and I'd value your opinion on them. That will be done when we go to West Virginia. Tex asked that I only bring four guards here, so that the clan wouldn't be alarmed by it. As long as things go smoothly we're only here until the day after tomorrow, so having four guards shouldn't be a problem."

"Is she aware of the security threats that surround her? To be frank, I need to know if she's going to fight the guards protecting her, or if she'll let us to our job."

"She'll let you do what you need to do, I'll make sure of it. Any problems arise, you let me know." Jinx slipped his cowboy hat off and sat it on the table. "I was thinking of Carson for your second, is that okay with you?"

Jackson nodded. "He's a good man. I understand you want what was said here quiet until Tabitha makes her announcement, but I feel that Carson needs to be aware of it to perform his duties to the best of his abilities."

"I agree, fill him in and then get some sleep." Jinx stood up from the table. "I want you and Carson back here at eight tomorrow morning. I have some things I need to take care of and I want someone watching my family. They're not to be cooped up. If Summer wants to take Claire out, that's fine as long as two guards are with them."

"Understood. I'll see you in the morning."

Jinx rolled his shoulders. Exhaustion had begun to set in, but he still had to finish things with Lukas before sleep could be considered. Turning to his brother, he felt his stomach twist as he wondered when the answer would come about the Lieutenant position.

Chapter Fourteen

Jinx sat there listening to Lukas go over the rest of the security details, but he was completely uninterested. For the first time in longer than he could remember he wasn't interested in the figures, or what was happening. He just wanted to know if Lukas was going to take the position. He started to ask him but each time he bit his tongue.

Knowing his brother as he did, he was aware that pressing him would only delay the answer. Lukas needed time to work things out for himself. He had never been one that could be pressured into something, and he never let family or friends sway his decision. It was one of the things that made Jinx want Lukas as his Lieutenant.

"Jinx…" Lukas waved a hand in front of Jinx's face, and it was clear that he had missed something. "You're not even listening to me."

"I apologize, Lukas, that was rude of me. To say I have a lot on my mind would be an understatement, and though true, it's no excuse. I should have been paying attention."

"Thinking about your mate? I know I'm keeping you from her, but I thought you wanted me to go over this stuff to bring you up to date."

"Summer is always on my mind. You'll find out just how much your mate is in your thoughts once you're mated." He shook his head. "That wasn't what I was thinking about now. Beyond what my tiger is telling me, there is more to life than just mating." Since finding Summer, his tiger had paced within him, always demanding he touch her, then never being satisfied when he did. The tiger always wanted more, more of his mate, more of everything.

Lukas leaned back against the sofa and stretched his legs out. "Would it help if I said I was considering your offer?"

Years of training were the only thing that kept what he was feeling from showing on his face. That and the fact he didn't know if he should be smiling or frowning. Lukas was too hard to read for Jinx to get a clear picture of what he was thinking.

"I guess that depends on which way you are considering it." He couldn't help but let out a nervous laugh. This could be the moment that defined things between them. "Are you considering telling me to screw off and shove the clan? Or are you interested in the position?"

"I'd be lying if I said I wasn't interested."

Jinx could feel there was a *but* coming, even when Lukas remained silent. "But?"

"My time in Alaska allowed me to discover me. I love working with Connor, and I'm good at it. I can put my skills to use and help our kind."

"The Nerd Crew won you over."

Lukas shook his head. "That's not what I'm saying. While you were downstairs I had an interesting conversation with your lass."

He wasn't thrilled that Summer and Lukas had been talking about the decision while he was away. It was Lukas's decision to make and he didn't want her pressuring him just to make him happy.

"I hope she didn't press you into anything."

"No pressure. She suggested we find a middle ground and compromise." Lukas smiled. "So if this compromising crap doesn't work, then you know who to blame. You're sweet lass has a way of making you believe things will work out."

"I believe I'll be having a word with my mate later. Alphas do not compromise well, neither do stubborn little brothers."

"Well, let's go against everything in us and at least try it, for our sake and the sake of the clan. What do you say? It's worth a try, isn't it?"

"Fine." He wasn't sure he liked it, but it couldn't hurt. "Put your cards on the table and we'll go from there."

"I'm not asking much." Lukas leaned forward, resting his elbows on his knees. "I'll take the position if I can continue working with Connor remotely. I'm useful there, and you know Ty needs all the help he can get when it comes to the Nerd Crew."

"What about when I'm away? How are you going to balance the responsibilities of the Nerd Crew with your duty to the clan? How long until one begins to suffer, and when that happens, which one will be neglected?"

"I can do both. I'll work it out with Connor and Ty. You know I can do this." He dragged his hand over his face. "Damn it, the clan means everything to me just like it does you. I wouldn't neglect them, and you know it. This can work if you just give a little. Everything I do for Connor and Ty can be done from anywhere."

"What about the commitments you made to Tex? The website?"

"Come on, Jinx. You know that's not going to be anything time consuming. Hell, you could do it in your sleep."

"There's a reason I don't do the computer stuff any longer. It's too time consuming with my duties as an Alpha." There were days when he missed geeking it out with Lukas but those days were in the past. He had responsibilities to his clan, to Ty, to Tex, and now a family.

"That's because you were trying to do it all on your own. Even small clans are starting to promote Lieutenants so the Alpha isn't doing everything. What about Eric? What if I bring him on to help with the Nerd Crew duties, the website for Tex? I'll oversee him, and pick and choose the projects I work on personally but at least my hand is still in it."

"Eric is good, but he doesn't have your skills." Jinx thought about Eric. He was a true computer geek, and it showed in everything from the way he talked to his clothes. He was a good kid, if someone that was twenty-two was even considered a kid.

"He has the skills. With some direction he'll pick up on what he doesn't know. The website won't be any problem for him."

"I'm not concerned about the website." He stood and paced the room, careful to avoid the piles of Summer's belongings. "He can't do much until Tabitha makes her announcement, and he'd have to be approved by Connor and Ty. You get them to approve him and it's fine by me. Otherwise if you take the position you're going to have to cut down on what you do for them. You put in long hours on the computer, it's not something you can do full time along with the clan duties you'll have."

"See, I was right, a compromise wasn't so bad," a soft feminine voice intoned.

Jinx turned to find Summer standing in the doorway in a pair of plaid pajama bottoms and a black tank top, her wet hair curling slightly.

"What, you didn't expect me to miss everything, did you?" She smirked.

He held his arm out to her; she came and snuggled next to him and he turned his attention back to Lukas. "Does that mean you're going to take the position?"

"I wanted to say yes when you offered it, I just didn't want to give up everything I've been working for these last few months." Lukas smiled at them and gave a little nod. "With your agreement that I can work with Connor as long as it doesn't interfere with my clan duties, then yes, I'll take it."

"You have my word, but the first sign of neglect when it comes to the clan, you give up your Nerd Crew duties. Understand?"

Lukas stood. "Yes."

"Very well." He slipped his arm out from around her and held his hand out to Lukas. "You'll need to come home to West Virginia with us, and we'll announce it then."

Once they shook hands, Summer beamed at him. "Congratulations. I told you it would work out."

"That you did." He stepped back, gathering up his stuff. "I'll let you get some rest. We'll have a lot to do to get things finished for us to leave." Lukas strolled from the suite, leaving them alone.

"Let's go to bed." He slid his hand down her body, pulled her close, and slipped beneath the material of her pajamas.

"Oh no, none of that. We've got a sleeping little girl in our room," she reminded him.

"I just want to feel you next to me." He took her hand, tugging her to the bedroom.

* * *

While snuggling with her mate, she couldn't believe how quickly things had changed. Weeks ago she had been a prisoner, scared of everything, now here she was full of life and love. She had a mate she adored with all her heart, and a daughter she was devoted to.

"What's on your mind, lass?"

She cradled her head in the nook of his arm and looked up at him. "I'm just appreciating how everything turned out. I have to say I wanted to but never believed Autumn when she said Tex would come back for us. He's made sure we were safe."

"Why?"

"I guess I felt that if he had a chance to get away and put it all behind him that he'd take it. That he wouldn't risk coming back and getting stuck under Avery's thumb again, or worse yet…killed. I never thought he'd find people to help him free the clan." She let out a deep sigh. "I guess with all I saw, I lost faith in people. That was until I found you. Now I believe there's good in people. That others will do the right thing."

He ran his hand down her arm in long lazy circles. "I'll be honest, some days it seems like an endless battle, that there's more bad than good in the world. When I see how far people have come after our help, I can't help but feel honored to have a part in it."

"I heard Tex putting straight one of the clan members today. I guess some believed that you and Ty were overthrowing all the Alphas who were against you and putting your own people there instead."

"Yeah, Tex told me about that. You know it's not true, right?" He didn't want her to answer. "The Ohio clan was being abused just as you were. You haven't met him yet, but Felix is Tabitha's Captain of the Guards. His brother was in Ohio suffering their tortures. It's how we found out, and part of the reason Korbin is now Ohio's Alpha. Under Korbin's command, the Ohio clan has come a long way. They are even planning to open a resort like Manetka, but on a much smaller scale."

"I knew you and Ty weren't the type to overthrow other Alphas."

She snuggled deeper against Jinx, letting her hand run down his chest, feeling the muscles constrict under her touch. He was everything she needed, and more she didn't even know she wanted.

She wanted to lose herself in his embrace, to forget everything that happened and seize what her future held. Her last day under Avery's rule would haunt her until she died, but she had to put it behind her for the sake of her family.

Chapter Fifteen

The next day and a half flew by, leaving Summer wishing for more time. She had been running around trying to get everything done, make progress with Claire, checking on a few people close to her, and still deal with packing. It left her exhausted and glad to be about to board the plane for West Virginia.

The only good thing that had come out of the last forty-eight hours was Claire had made some progress especially where Ben, Jinx, and surprisingly Jackson were concerned. There was something about Jackson's voice that the little girl loved. She'd bring him a book, and force him to hold her while he read it. It was sweet seeing Claire climb into Jackson's strong arms. She looked so small and fragile in the big man's lap. Even with the progress Claire had made, she had yet to speak.

There on the landing strip was where everything was going to change. Summer stood with a very sleepy Claire on her hip, about to board a plane to take her to her new clan. Never again would this be her home. She might be welcomed at the resort, but it would never be her clan again. West Virginia was about to be.

Or I guess it already is since I'm Alpha Female to the clan.

She pushed her thoughts away, and tried not to dwell on the negative.

"I'm going to miss you," Ben said, giving her a hug.

Feeling Ben's arms around her almost made her lose it. He had been her protector for years, and now she was leaving him to go to the other side of the country. It didn't matter that they would visit, or that she could have the clan's private plane bring her here anytime she wanted. All that mattered was she was leaving him, and it was breaking her heart.

"Don't cry. This isn't goodbye. I'm going to see you soon for Tabitha's announcement." He playfully tugged Claire's thumb out of her mouth. "Same with you, little one. You're going to remember your Uncle Ben when I see you in a few weeks, aren't you?"

She nodded, her little hand reaching out to cup his cheek. When he leaned closer she kissed him. It was a perfect ending to their days in Texas.

"I couldn't have asked for a better goodbye." He kissed Claire's cheek before looking back up at her. "I love you, and if you ever need anything day or night you can call me. Got it?"

She nodded and wrapped her arms around him. "I love you too."

"Lass…" Jinx stepped away from where he'd been talking to Tex, and walked over to her. "We should go."

"What about Ashley? Isn't she coming?"

Tex moved up to stand next to Ben. "We decided it was best for Claire that she doesn't. Next visit we can try again, but right now Claire is making progress and none of us want to set it back."

"I'm doubtful Ashley went along with it quietly."

"She was upset but finally agreed. It might be nice if you consider emailing her pictures of Claire from time to time," Tex suggested.

"Okay. I also promised I'd call her with updates. I don't want to take Claire away from her family. I only want to do what's right for her."

"That's what we all want, lass," Jinx reassured her.

"Carson and Garth are already on board," Lukas told Jinx when he came to stand by them. "Tex, if anything comes up with the security, let me know, otherwise Larry can finish what needs to be done and can handle most problems."

"Very good. Thank you for all you've done for my clan." Tex held out his hand and Lukas shook it.

"My pleasure."

"Larry's staying?" Summer asked, feeling like she missed a shred of something.

"With Lukas stepping up as my Lieutenant, he won't be able to stay here. So for a few weeks, Larry's going to be here, and we'll get you a replacement guard until he returns." Jinx slipped his arm around her, and Claire pressed her hand against him. "We'll see you again soon, and if anything should arise you know how to reach me."

Summer pushed the tears away and swallowed the lump that had formed in her throat. With one last halfhearted smile, she let Jinx lead her up the steps and into the plane, Jackson and Lukas at their heels.

"I know your heart is breaking because I can feel the pain as if it was my own," Jinx said, his voice soft. "Distance isn't going to change things with you and Ben. He'll still come running if you need him. The bond between you isn't one that will be broken easily."

"It's just so sad." She let herself take comfort from his embrace. "I'll be okay. I know you need to get to the cockpit."

"Actually, I'm going to let Lukas handle this one. My family needs me more." He led her to one of the small sofas. Sliding into their seats, he put his arm around her and let her snuggle against him. "Everything is going to be fine."

"I know." Claire snuggled between them, half on each of their legs, nearly asleep. "Claire must think so too, or she just has faith we can protect her from anything that might come up." She nodded to their now sleeping daughter.

"She knows we wouldn't allow anything to happen to her." His finger teased along Summer's jawline, bringing her face to his and kissing her. When the kiss ended, their faces still close, he whispered. "You should get some sleep, you've been doing too much lately."

"I'm not tired…"

* * *

The plane touched down but Jinx couldn't bring himself to wake Summer until the last moment. She looked so peaceful sleeping there with Claire curled around her. Their kind always enjoyed sleeping in a big pile.

"My sweet lass," he whispered, tucking a strand of her hair behind her ear.

"Umm."

"We're here, lass."

Her eyes shot open and she started to jump up before she realized Claire was on her lap. "Oh. I'm not ready."

"Lass…" He picked Claire up, careful not to wake her, and pulled Summer to her feet. "They're going to love you. Come meet our clan."

"I should freshen up."

"You look great. Now come on." He tugged her to the door and down the steps. Jackson and Carson stood at the bottom of the steps waiting for her. Everyone else stood gathered around the landing strip. "Look, everyone's here to meet you and Claire."

"Why?"

"Because this is your clan, you're Alpha Female. They are happy to have you here with us. Now come meet our family." Climbing down the steps, be felt like the world was his. He had everything anyone could ever want. In that moment he didn't worry about the rogues that were still out there, or the future of their kind. He only enjoyed what he had with him.

"They're all here," Summer mumbled, stifling a yawn.

"We'll go inside to the ballroom, that's where we'll make our announcements and mingle," Jinx said. "We have a busy few hours ahead of us while every tries to get a moment with you. I hope you are up to it."

"I'll be fine." She glanced at Claire in his arms. "Wonder if she's going to be okay with so many new people."

"If it becomes too much, we'll end it. I think she'll be fine as long as we're with her. She's going to have to get used to the clan. This is her home now. Our home." He squeezed his arm around her waist tighter and they descended the stairs.

At the bottom of the stairs, with Carson on his right and Jackson on the other side of Summer, he stopped. "I'd like to thank everyone for coming out on this cold evening to welcome Summer and Claire to the clan. I ask that we make our way into the ballroom. I have a couple announcements, and then I promise we'll mingle giving everyone a chance to meet her." Some of the ground guards began to urge everyone toward the ballroom.

Summer glanced over the land, surprised how much it reminded her of Texas with the farms surrounding it, and the rolling hills of endless space. The biggest difference was the cold. It was freezing. They arrived at the perfect time. The sun was just setting, casting an exquisite glow of reds and yellows over the area.

"I can't believe I didn't ask before. Where are we?" Summer wondered.

"Just outside of Snowshoe, West Virginia. We own over nine hundred and fifty acres."

Still glancing around, she tipped her head to the side. "Almost a thousand acres? How do you keep it all safe?"

"There are guard houses around the perimeter, where guards are always stationed. Every piece of the board is covered with motion sensors, heat sensors, and cameras. No one can get on or off the property without us being alerted. There is also a second layer of security once you've come onto the property," Lukas explained.

"We are far enough way from any roads or houses that we are never bothered," Jinx interjected. "You can't just stumble upon this place, you have to know what you're looking for to end up here. The guards are well trained and protect the border and the clan." Jinx led them forward at a slower place so they could keep their distance from the stragglers making their way into the ballroom. "Our homes are built in the center of the land, at the safest point. That building you see just ahead on the hill is ours. From there, we can see almost the whole compound."

The building he indicated was huge. It was a three-story log home, towering over all the others. A beautiful winding pathway led to the houses below, with shrubs that appeared to be the kind that would flower in the summer.

"That can't be just for us." Summer gasped.

"I have taken my quarters on the third floor. Lukas will once again take over the second, and Jackson, I'd like for you and Carson to make your residence on the first floor."

"Yes, sir. We'll see to that once we have you and your family safely home for the evening," Jackson replied, his gaze scanning the area for any possible threats.

"Wow." It was hard to believe she was about to live in that house. It seemed like too much just for them. "Doesn't the clan ever have a problem with you towering above them like that? Like you're watching their every move?"

"It has been like that for centuries. The Alpha is in charge of their safety and the house allows me to watch over the land, and spot threats before they can get close enough to do us any harm," he explained. "I have no interest in spying on my members, and before I started traveling to Alaska I was only in the house to sleep. You'll find the clan is always gathered. This building we are going to has a ballroom for special occasions, parties, weddings, that type of thing. It also has a large dining area that will fit all the members. At least weekly, we take our meals together as a family. We're very close."

"You mentioned that, but I guess I didn't believe there could ever be a closeness in a clan like you described."

"Trust me, lass, there is and you're about to see it. Remember, I told you we believe it takes a clan to raise a child, well that doesn't change with families. Everyone is always in everyone's business, it's just how we are. I might be Alpha of the clan, but they are still in my business." He let out a light laugh, the first one she heard that was truly joyful. He was glad to be home. It showed in every part of him.

"They've never considered me higher than they are," he continued, "and I don't want them to. I've always lived by the rule, never ask someone to do something you wouldn't do yourself. It's why I have almost every clan male as a willing guard. They know I wouldn't risk their lives if I wouldn't do the same, or if I felt like it was a battle we wouldn't win. The women's rights movement is just now trying to work its way through the clan."

"Just now?" She couldn't keep the surprise out of her voice.

"The clan mainly keeps to our land. We grow and raise our own food. Very rarely do any of us venture off the land. Some of the guards have gone on missions since we've started working with the Alaskan Tigers, but before that we were homebodies. Shifters have always protected the women and children. They are the key to allowing our species to continue." He paused as they neared the entry to the ballroom. "Our protection of women and children make it hard for women to be guards, or anything that puts their lives in danger. Too many of the men would stop what they were doing and would go to protect the women. It's too far engrained in us. Ty has a woman guard, Shadow, and she's the Captain of Bethany's guards, but in all the clans I know, she's the only one and it took her years to prove herself."

"If given the chance, others can as well."

"I agree, but to give them a chance the men must be willing to accept a woman can handle herself. Any woman guard would have to prove herself before she would be allowed to risk herself. Otherwise, too many could die." He laid his hand on her arm. "I realize it sounds like I live in a cave, and I'm not willing to give women a chance, but that isn't the case. I've seen what Shadow can do and I'd go into battle with her any day."

"But things will change when she's mated, won't they?"

He frowned at her. "That's not my place to say, it would be Ty's decision."

"If she was your guard?"

"Yes, things would change. I wouldn't risk a possibly pregnant female. If fertile, she'd be able to bring more generations to us. Too many shifters have problems conceiving, and of those cubs who are born over half of them don't make it past their second birthday. I won't stand by and see our numbers shrink and end our species if I can help it."

The reasons were logical, and the future of the clan and their species depended on new life being brought into the clan. In the human world, women were being allowed in the front lines of military operations where it had been forbidden in the past. They'd come a long way.

But in the shifter world, women were in the dark ages, after centuries of being taught woman should be protected, cherished, and that they were the key to the future. They couldn't protect their clan; instead they were expected to stay behind where it was safe.

"Being an Elder isn't easy," Jinx said. "There are hard decisions to make, ones that are going to upset people, but each decision has to be made in the best interest of the clan. Keeping women out of the front lines is in the best interest of the clan. We have come so far, and there's a brighter future ahead for all of us once we get through this."

"There are always dead in war," Summer countered. "If a woman is skilled and strong enough to defend the clan in battle, I believe she should."

"Which is why I would go into battle with Shadow. Don't think that she just came into her position. It has taken her years to prove herself. There are others who are trying, one actually I want you to meet." He adjusted Claire in his arms. "I'm willing to give them a chance if I think they can do it. I hold the men to the same condition. There are some guards I feel should remain ground guards, and others I would trust your safety to because of their skills. Women should be held to those standards too."

Jinx's Mate: Alaskan Tigers

Chapter Sixteen

As she listened to him, Summer realized Jinx would be open to the right woman guard. He wasn't one to risk someone that wasn't ready. He needed to have complete confidence in her, and the men working with her needed to be prepared to let her do what she needed to do.

"This woman you want me to meet?"

"She has aspirations of being a guard. Like Shadow she has been working her way up. Currently she is a grounds guard, closest to the homes. She has the skills, and desire to do it, she just needs to be given a chance in order to develop the instincts that come along with it." He took a step forward, once again moving them toward the door.

"Wait." She grabbed his arm, stopping him. "What do you expect me to do when I meet her?"

"See what you think of her." He glanced at Jackson. "We've considered the possibility of having her as one of your guards. Jackson has done some of her training and believes she's up for the challenge. Jackson and Carson can give her more of the training she needs without risking you or anyone else. She just needs to start trusting her instincts. Jackson can help hone those skills. Right now I want you to see what you think of her before we consider it further."

"You're going to have *me* make the decision? To be the woman's only chance…and if I say no, is that it for her?" She was worried she would think the guard had possibilities but wasn't ready yet, and then the woman would lose her chance. After all, Summer didn't mind a fresh guard when it came to her, but for Claire's safety she wasn't willing to risk it.

"It's not her only chance," Jinx clarified. "Jackson and I believe she would be a good fit, but I want to make sure you're comfortable. Any guards that are assigned to your protection are also in charge of protecting Claire, so you need to consider that was well. She has taken to Jackson, puts up with Carson, but she doesn't like Larry."

Her thoughts traveled back to Larry. He seemed to be a good guy, and an excellent guard, but he reminded her too much of Avery. Not in personality but in looks, and that could be what scared Claire. Their little lass must have seen some of the horrible things that were done to her mother. Did Avery make Claire watch while her mother was tortured? She hated the thought, but wouldn't put it past Avery; it was just like him to do something like that in an attempt to emotionally scar Claire.

"What are we going to do about Larry?"

"He's a good guard, one that I'd trust your safety to if I was called away. I want him a part of the team. Claire does okay as long as he isn't too close and they're not alone together. I think with time she'll warm up to him once she sees he has a soft side."

Tipping her head back, she laughed at the idea. "Where? He's all muscles, orders, and duty. Hell, I don't think I've seen him smile once."

"Okay, so it's hidden." Jinx's grinned. "Now come on, it's cold. Let's get this night train rolling so I can get you to myself." He nodded to Carson who pulled the door open.

Jackson stepped into the room first, with them following, Carson and Lukas taking up the rear. Everyone was already in their seats at the small tables around the room. They glanced at them as the pair made their way down the aisle with the guards. She felt as if she was about to be on trial.

She took a deep breath, trying to push away her fears as they turned to face the audience. Jinx gave her comfort with his arm around her waist, as did Jackson's presence beside her. She wished she was holding Claire. It would give her something to do with her hands. Something to focus on.

"It is my honor and privilege to introduce my mate, Summer, and our daughter Claire. As the parents in the room will understand, sometimes children fall asleep at the worst times." Jinx chuckled. "Claire has been through a lot recently and hasn't been sleeping very well. Now before we mingle so you can meet the new Alpha Female, there are a few announcements that need to be made."

"Do you want me to take her?" She whispered when Jinx nodded for Lukas to come forward.

"Not on your life. She's sleeping, and after last night I won't have her woken."

That sent chills through her. Last night had been the worst one yet for little Claire. She had woken from a nightmare, screaming. Jackson who was asleep across the hall came running half naked with his gun in hand. He stood in the doorway, looking for something he could kill, anything he could do to stop her from shrieking, but there was nothing. Clearly pained that he could do nothing to help Claire, Jackson left them alone. Whatever Avery did to her or her mother was haunting her dreams. Because she wouldn't talk, there was little they could do, so Summer and Jinx had taken her to bed with them and cuddled her close.

Summer blinked the memory away and returned to the present despite her exhaustion.

"Everyone here knows my brother Lukas," Jinx continued. "You also know he has been spending time in Alaska, helping the clan their with their computer needs. Being that most of it has been confidential, that is all any of us can tell you." He paused, waiting for Lukas to step up next to him. "However, while I was away, things have changed. Lukas will now take over the newly created position as the clan's Lieutenant."

A round of applaud and hollers of *way to go* and *congratulations* followed until Lukas raised his hand, silencing the room. "Thank you everyone, it is an honor to step into his position. I hope I will make everyone proud."

"Lukas is going to do a fine job, and having him here will make me confortable when I need to travel," Jinx said. "One more announcement before we let the evening's activities begin. Because I have a family now, it is time to assign Elder guards to our protection. Jackson has agreed to come on as Summer's Captain of the Guards, with Carson as his second. Claire is young and won't be leaving Summer's side, at least not until we've worked through her fears. So I'm not permanently assigning guards to her yet. Summer's guards will protect her as well."

"How long are you home for?" a man at the first table asked.

"Uncle Tony, I'll be home as long as I can. We need to take Claire to see someone in Alaska who believes she might be able to help Claire overcome her past."

"She doesn't need a therapist, all she needs is family," a woman called from somewhere in the room.

"I won't go into details about it, but I will tell you this. Claire spent her whole life locked in a room below ground. Until two days ago she had never been around people, felt the sun on her face, the grass under her feet. She has been doing well as long as Summer is there, and she has taken a liking to Jackson and me, but we will still need to take things slow with her. If tonight becomes too much then we'll have to leave."

Summer cleared her throat, and gained everyone's attention. "Claire has seen more than some of us have seen our whole lives. She's frightened and we have to do what's right for her. I've seen Robin, and the therapist get others to open up to her. If there's a slight chance she can help my daughter, I'll do whatever I can to make sure she's seen."

"Maybe children of her own age would be good for her," the woman suggested.

Jinx leaned close to Summer and whispered, "Angie."

"Angie, it is possible and like Jinx said, we will do whatever we can for Claire, and explore each option," Summer told her. "I do want Claire to begin to meet some of the clan members and children her own age. Having a playmate would be good for her, as long as there's an understanding that right now Claire needs it in small doses. She hasn't spoken since she was freed. That might be hard on another child. I'm asking you give us a few days, let us get Claire settled in, and we'll slowly begin introducing her to everyone."

"I know parents with children Claire's age. We'll set up play dates as soon as we feel she's ready," Jinx added. "We don't want to keep her isolated, it's not good for her or us. We just want to take things slow. I'll appreciate if everyone respects that."

"We only want to do what's right by Claire." Summer smiled at the crowd, hoping they could understand where she was coming from.

"Now that the announcements are done. How about we get this party started?" Excitement laced Jinx's voice. "Summer and I will be making our way around, trying to spend a few minutes with each of you. Remember tonight is about having a little fun, meeting the new Alpha Female, and tomorrow we'll worry about work and everything else."

While he addressed the clan, she was awed by the change in him. There was always authority seeping from him, but among his clan there was also a relaxed sense to him. He loved being home, back in charge of his clan. He might have be comfortable in Texas, but not like this.

"Are you ready to meet the clan, lass?" He held out his arm to her.

"As ready as I'll ever be." She smirked and laced her arm through his. "I just wish Claire could be awake for this."

"Maybe it's for the best. All these people in one place might be too much for her. With her sleeping, you'll be able to meet people without her clinging to you in fear."

"Instead you have to carry her around."

"That's what fathers are for." He teased. "Just wait until boys start coming around."

"We're shifters, they don't come around like humans."

"Not like humans, no, but we sniff around you girls once we start wondering where are mate is. She'll have boys coming out of the woodwork to see if she's their mate. All the while I'll be cleaning my shotgun." Summer raised an eyebrow at him and he continued to smirk at her. "Fine, not a shotgun, but my pistol will do the job."

"You will not kill our daughter's mate," she warned.

"I'll take your wishes into consideration when the time comes." He led her over to the first table where his Uncle Tony sat. "Come on, Uncle Tony will get upset if I don't introduce him first."

"It's about time my nephew finds his mate." He stood up, quickly wrapping his arms around her in a hug. "Welcome to the family. Maybe you can get this wandering Alpha to settle down and stay home for a change."

How did Jinx deal with people questioning why he was away when they couldn't tell anyone the true reason? She just smiled. "I'll see what I can do, after we take Claire to Alaska."

"Angie's right, we can help her."

"Uncle, we'll give the clan a chance as well," Jinx interjected. "I know you're not fond of doctors, but like when I brought on the clan's doctor, I believe it can be of help to Claire. You don't have to agree but it's our decision to give it a try."

"It's a waste." Tony gave Summer a meaningful glance. "Go mingle. I'll be seeing you later."

Chapter Seventeen

The evening had been a fun filled and somewhat overwhelming experience. Now all Summer wanted to do was curl up next to Jinx. Claire had woken up halfway through the evening and though she'd been scared with all the new people gathered around, she did fine once Summer held her. Everything had fallen into place. Even the clan's emotions had categorized themselves just as he had predicted, and were no longer overwhelming, leaving her free to focus on Jinx's wants and needs.

She stepped up next to him, slipping her hand into his. "Can we go now?"

"Almost, lass. Jackson, can you stop Meshell before she leaves? I want Summer to meet her before we leave."

"Tonight?" Even as she asked it, Jackson stepped away from them, going back to the table where Lukas was sitting with a couple guys and two women.

"What better time? First impressions can be a world of good. In the morning, Carson will put her through her paces for you. Then if you are still interested, we can meet with her again."

She didn't bother to argue, only sat down and adjusted Claire so she was sitting on her legs. "My sweet little girl, I'm going to get muscles as big as Jinx's if I have to keep carrying you around."

"Speaking of that. Robin suggested that since the paperwork was drawn up before we left Texas, we can make the adoption official." He sat down next to them, putting his hand over theirs. "Maybe we should refer to ourselves as proper parents, that way when she starts talking she'll know what to call us."

"You mean like Mom and Dad?"

"Exactly. It might be easier for her, especially once we have kids of our own. We don't want her to feel like she isn't as much a part of our life and love as they are."

She ran her thumb over Jinx's hand and looked down at Claire. "Would you like that, Claire? Do you want us to be your Mommy and Daddy?"

Before Claire could answer, not that Summer really expected her to, Jackson had returned with a woman. Her long black hair and deep chocolate brown eyes were the first features Summer noticed about her.

"Summer, this is Meshell." Jackson introduced them.

"Meshell, please have a seat." Jinx nodded to the seat across from them. "I was telling Summer that you're one of the ground guards here, and I wanted to introduce you both since you seemed to have been missing part of the evening."

"I was patrolling." She pulled out the chair and sat down. "Most of the guards covered for each other so we could be here. By the time I got here you were already eating. I didn't want to interrupt." It was painfully clear that Meshell was nervous, even slightly uncomfortable being singled out.

Summer watched how the woman moved. She was extremely fit, but not overly that took her to an unattractive level. Underneath, the womanhood was still clear. "How do you enjoy working with the clan?" Summer asked.

"I love it. It's been what I've worked for my whole life."

Claire begun squirming in Summer's lap and rubbing her eyes. "We're almost done, sweetie."

"Someone is tired." Meshell smiled at Claire.

"It's been a long few days for all of us, especially Claire," Jinx confirmed. "I wanted to give Summer time to get to know you, but I'm afraid Claire has other ideas."

"I understand. There will be other times." She nodded and stood. "Welcome to the clan."

When Meshell walked away, he turned to Summer. "Sorry, lass, but I believe we've pushed Claire as far as we can tonight. Let's get her home."

In agreement, she let him take Claire from her and stood. There would always be tomorrow to see if Meshell could cut it as one of the Elder guards.

* * *

The hour was early with darkness still surrounding the West Virginia land when the alarms were going off. Jinx hurried out of bed, slipping into a pair of jeans and grabbing the gun he had at the bedside table. The easy reach of the weapon reminded him that he'd have to lock up his guns now that Claire was in the house.

"What's going on?" Summer asked, fear creeping in her voice.

"Someone or something has crossed the perimeter. I'm sure Jackson and Carson are on their way up. I'll have to check it out."

"I'll go check on Claire." She grabbed the yoga pants and tank top she'd thrown at the end of the bed. With Claire sleeping soundly in the next room, they'd been able to enjoy each other's company before falling asleep the night before.

"You don't have to worry about her," Jinx promised. "The building is safe and she's probably sleeping. Nothing can get in, not with everything locked down for the night."

"If she hears the alarm, she'll be frightened." Summer tugged the tank top over her head.

The elevator ding let them know someone had arrived.

"Jinx. Carson and I are here," Jackson called out as they stepped off the elevator.

"I'll be back." Jinx crossed the room. "If anything happens, stay with them."

"Be safe," she whispered as he dashed out.

On his way, he glanced at the guards. "Summer's going to check on Claire. If anything happens you know what to do." Knowing the men would keep her safe, he didn't wait for a reply, just stepped onto the elevator and left.

The elevator stopped on the second floor and Lukas stepped in, still getting dressed. "What the hell's going on?"

"I don't know, but I'll tell you this. First thing tomorrow your first assignment is to get us those ear transmitters Ty's clan has. It would make this easier. At the moment, we're heading out blind." He growled, not know what was happening at the perimeter.

"I left the ATV just outside the front doors last night after my perimeter check." Lukas tossed the keys to him and shoved on his sweatshirt.

"Good." Jinx caught the keys midair. "While I'm giving you duties, I want two guards outside the house at night, and I want you to find yourself Elder guards."

"But I don't have a mate. I don't need them," Lukas argued.

"You know what's coming as much as I do. You'll have guards on standby for when they are needed. I won't have you killed because of an oversight." The elevator doors opened and Jinx ran full speed through the entryway to the front door and out to the ATV.

The ATV roared to life. A split second later, Lukas jumped on board and they were hurling down the path to where the alarm had sounded. Around the houses, and through the trees before he could open it up completely. The cold night air and snowflakes nipped at Jinx's naked chest, but he barely realized it; all he cared about was getting to wherever the threat was. No one would be screwing up his mate's first night with the clan, or putting the fear back into Claire.

With a wave of his arm, a guard at the inner perimeter stopped them.

"What?" Jinx barked, irritated.

"It's a bear, animal not shifter, and they've dealt with it."

"Damn it. Is no one marking the territory? We shouldn't have animals traipsing through the area if it was marked properly."

"I can't answer that, sir." The guard shrugged. "It hasn't been one of my assigned duties. I believe the front line handles it."

"I'll see to it in the morning, and make sure everything is marked," Lukas told him. "Let's get back to the house. We'll let the guards and Summer know everything is safe."

"Richard, isn't it?" Jinx wasn't sure in the darkness.

"Yes, sir."

With no desire to make the trip to the perimeter and back, he sent Richard instead. "Go tell them I've been alerted of the issue and they are to report to the meeting room at nine o'clock."

"Very well, sir." Richard hopped onto his own ATV and took off.

"Add marking the territory to your list," Jinx told Lukas. "I want you to make sure it's done by nightfall. I do not want a rehash of this again." He turned the ATV around and started heading back to the house. "See what I mean about the hours you'll put in for the clan?"

"I understand, and can still do everything. I've made arrangements for Eric to accompany us when we go to Alaska. We'll only be away two days, so don't worry about the clan. Eric and I will fly out with you. I'll get Ty to approve Eric, and then we'll fly back the next day. Everything will be fine."

"For your sake and sanity, I hope Ty will approve Eric. If not, you're going to be exhausted rather quickly."

"There's no need to worry, he will. Eric has the skills Ty needs and with me overseeing everything there won't be a problem. I can do this. Just have a little faith in me."

He took his gaze off the path for a moment and glanced at Lukas. "I've always had faith in you or I wouldn't have asked you to be my Lieutenant." The ATV came to a halt in front of the house where lights gleamed from the third floor. Before he went inside there was one thing he wanted Lukas's opinion on. "You've had some contact with Meshell in her guard duties."

"Very little, why?"

"I'm considering adding her to the team to protect Summer and Claire. She'd be the additional guard for the time being, always the third on when guarding my family. Jackson believes if we give her a chance she'll live up to the task."

"But you're worried."

"I have confidence in Meshell when it comes to ground duties, even considered moving her to the outer perimeter, but this is my family we're talking about. I won't risk them."

Lukas turned slightly to look over at Jinx. "If you think Meshell is up for it, do it on a trial run. Always keep her with guards you know will protect Summer and Claire no matter what happens. Even use her only here on our land, where the security is higher, at least at first. I have to agree with Jackson, she could be a good guard with a little more training, and having another woman around might be good for Claire."

"So you think I should try Meshell?" He had a feeling Lukas would say that.

"I've seen her in training and when on duty. She's dedicated, the skills are there, and she cares about the clan. All qualities in a good guard." Lukas nodded. "What does Summer think?"

He shut off the ATV and glanced up to the third floor. "She met her at the end of the night, but it wasn't enough for much. Poor Claire was done, she had enough of meeting everyone and we had to leave. Jackson is going to put Meshell through her paces this morning, giving Summer a chance to observe. Then they can meet again if Summer finds her acceptable."

"I don't believe Jackson is putting her through the paces just for Summer. It's for you too. You need that final push to convince you she's ready." Lukas stepped off, stretching his legs as Jinx came around. "If you don't want to risk her with your family, I'll take her as one of my guards. It will give her the chance."

"If I feel she's not ready for Summer and Claire, I'm certainly not allowing her to guard you. If she's not ready, we can move her to the outer perimeter and go from there. Maybe in a few months she'll be ready for the next step." He climbed the couple steps to the deck, Lukas behind him. "Now get some sleep. You have a lot to attend to in the morning."

"Goodnight. I'll lock up, you go to Summer."

He didn't argue. There was a bounce in his step and a lightness to his heart knowing that in just a few minutes he'd have his arms around Summer. No longer tired, he had another idea on how they could spend the rest of the night.

Jinx's Mate: Alaskan Tigers

Chapter Eighteen

The soft glow of the moon shone through the window, casting just enough light for Summer to watch Jackson with Claire. The sweet girl had been terrified when she woke to the alarm going off. Summer had calmed her but when Jackson stepped into the bedroom to check on them she held her arms out to him.

The reaction from Claire had both been joyful and painful for Summer. It was good to see Claire connecting with others, but at the same time painful because she didn't seem to want Summer to hold her.

In that instant she realized how blind she was in this parenthood. Normally parents, and the Elders, could feel a child's emotions just as the Elders did for all the clan members, but not with Claire. She had no commitments to the clan, no blood bond to anyone in the clan, making her an enigma.

The elevator ding sounded like a quarter dropping in a silent room, sending a wave a fear through her. Carson already had his gun trained on the door when Jackson stepped around her, putting himself in front of her and the doorway to Claire.

"I think it's Jinx," she whispered, afraid to speak any louder.

"It should be," he reassured her. "The elevator is only coded to open to those Jinx allows. The three of you, Lukas, Carson and me—no one else unless someone was able to override the system. With the triple steel doors that are supposed to withhold any attack, we can't smell anyone inside. Just stay back until we know for sure."

She glanced back at Claire, making sure she was still asleep, before turning her gaze back to the elevator doors. Never before had it taken an eternity for an elevator to go three floors, at least not until then.

The elevators opened and she heard Jinx's voice. "It's me and everything is under control." He stepped out of the elevator and Carson holstered his gun. "It was a bear."

Jackson moved aside and she went to him. "Animal or shifter?"

"Animal." He slipped his arm around her waist. "Seems while I was away some of the guards decided to slack on their duties marking the perimeter. I'll deal with them in the morning, and Lukas will see that the perimeter is marked. How's Claire?"

"Jackson got her back to sleep."

"Jackson?" He looked over at the Captain of the Guards. "Getting in some fatherly experience before it's your time? Don't blame you there."

"She's a sweet child, and surprisingly she took to me. I'm happy to do whatever I can to make things easier for her, and for both of you." Jackson stepped away from Claire's doorway. "Carson and I will leave now. If you need anything, we're just downstairs."

"Thank you." Jinx nodded and turned back to her. "Now as for you…" He reached down, scooping Summer into his arms, and carried her toward the bedroom.

"What are you doing? Put me down."

"I've been thinking about how much I want you, how I want to be buried deep within you." He laid her on the bed and tugged at the tank top she threw on.

"Who knew an alarm call in the middle of the night could turn into something so exciting?" She unbuttoned his jeans and let them fall away.

"Take off your pants," he ordered, pulling off his cowboy boots and stepping out of his jeans.

"That's my mate, always demanding."

"I can't help it if I like you naked, to feel your body against mine, bare skin to bare skin." He pounced on her, landing on top of her and pressing her back against the bed. "You're mine, now and always. I love you."

"I love you too." She slipped her hand between them, wrapping her hand around his shaft and applying just enough pressure that he arched over her. "I love that I have so much control over my big strong Alpha."

"When your hand is there…" The words stopped as her fingers slid down the length of him.

"Yes?"

"Doing that…ahhh…how could anyone resist you?" He leaned closer, pressing his lips to hers in a hungry kiss.

"Take me," she ordered. Their beasts mingled within them, caressing each other. No longer could she wait; she needed him like she needed her next breath.

Without breaking the kiss, he slid between her legs. His shaft teased along her folds before he gently pushed into her, bringing a moan to her lips. With his shaft buried deep within her, she felt whole. Their connection was taken to a whole new level. With each touch it sent pleasure shooting through her.

"Faster." She lifted her hips to meet his as he pumped into her.

"So demanding." With each stroke he brought it up another level, slowly intensifying the tempo until she was ready to roll him over and do it herself. When her control was almost at its limit, his hips slammed into her as she met each thrust.

"Come for me, lass. I want to feel your muscles tighten against me."

Minutes later, an orgasm coursed through her. Her body arched into him, nails digging into the soft skin of his back. "Ah, Jinx."

Seconds later he buried his head in her shoulder, growling her name as his own release followed. Nuzzling her neck, he stayed buried deep within her. "How did I ever get so lucky?" He kissed a line along her neck, working his way to her ear.

"If you keep doing that, I'm going to be ready for round two."

As if agreeing, his shaft twitched, hardening against the walls of her core. "Shifters are known for their stamina."

"Umm." She moaned, teasing her fingers along his sides. "You might be Mr. Eveready, but I do need a little recovery time."

She could feel a slight twinge of disappointment as he slid from her. He lay next to her, the length of his body pressed against her.

"There was something I wanted to ask you."

"For some reason, I have a feeling this isn't going to be sweet after-sex conversation."

She laced her fingers through his. "It's not bad, but not good either."

"Lass, I love when you narrow things down." He squeezed her hand. "Just get it out."

"I can't feel Claire like I can the other members. Can you?"

"No." He leaned up on his arm, and looked down at her, panic widening his eyes. "I had hoped to approach you about that now that we're here. I was hoping you'd established a bond with her."

Without trying, he had managed to bring all her fears to life. Their daughter was a mystery. One neither of them would be able to control if she ever went against them. They'd never know until it was too late.

"What are we going to do?"

"Raise her right." He caressed her thigh. "It's all we can do. Raise her right and hope for the best. When she's old enough to commit to the clan…"

"What if she won't? What then?" When he didn't answer, she watched him carefully. "Would you really force our daughter to leave the clan?"

"Oh, lass." He pulled her tight against him.

"You would, wouldn't you?" She blinked away the tears.

"It's not going to come to that."

"You don't know that. After everything she's seen…she could turn against us. Against us all." Thinking the little girl in the next room, so small and dependent, could one day turn against them broke her heart. It was the worse pain she ever felt, even worse then the day she lost Autumn. "Answer me, truthfully. You'd force her to leave the clan, wouldn't you? Our own daughter."

"The West Virginia Tigers have always been a little different. Many of our families stay together, stay here. We're a family clan." He paused, his lips curved down in a frown. "Even with all that and the love I already have for Claire, yes, I would. I wouldn't have a choice. We can't risk our whole clan, everyone that depends on us, for someone that is against us no matter who they are."

"What if she was our own flesh and blood?"

"We wouldn't have this issue with our flesh and blood, they would be connected to us from birth. There would never be a doubt of loyalty to us or the clan." He squeezed her hand. "I'm truly sorry but I can't give you the words you want to hear. I can only tell you that if we raise her right and do what we can to help her put the past behind her, we stand a good chance of never having to make that decision."

She wished that was enough to calm her, but it wasn't. If anything it frightened her, and made her want to question every decision she made. Would one of their decisions give Claire a reason to turn against them in the future?

* * *

Jinx sat in his home office dealing with clan business. Going over the things that had slipped to the side while he was in Alaska. So much work and so little time before they had to go back to Alaska. He had forced Lukas to choose between his duty to the clan and the Nerd Crew. Now Jinx had a feeling the day would soon arrive when he would have to make a similar choice.

His clan needed him here, and his family needed stability instead of always traveling, but on the other side of things Ty and Tabitha needed him. Somehow there had to be a balance. One that would allow him to be there for Tabitha and her new world, while still giving himself completely to his family and clan.

Suddenly his computer alerted him to a call from Ty through the secure computer transmissions that Lukas himself had coded. Leaning back against the leather chair he pushed the button, accepting the call. A brief moment later Ty's face filled the screen.

"What has you up and busy this early?"

Ty sat in his own home office, his shoulder length dark hair pulled back in a leather strap and worry lines creasing his face. "We received a call from Tex. Cliff attacked the compound last night with three other former clan members. They're dead."

"Is everyone in Texas okay? Ben?" The thought of telling his mate that her brother was injured or worse when they had just left the day before made him ill.

"Ben's fine. One of the guards was shot but he's going to be fine."

"Then I can't help but wonder why you called." Jinx tossed the pen he had been rolling between his hands on the desk.

"The Texas Tigers proved they are strong by overcoming their first attack. It was the final step needed. Tabitha will be making her announcement soon. We'd like for you to be here for it, and we need Lukas to patch into every clan's computer system for the announcement."

"I need time to put in place the final Elder guards for Summer and Claire, which I have planned for this evening. We could leave first thing in the morning if that's soon enough for you." He wasn't going to take Summer and Claire without additional guards to keep them safe.

"That will be fine." Ty nodded. "We'll set the announcement for the following day."

"I believe Lukas has already received your approval for Eric to join us. He's seeking to have Eric come on as one of the Nerd Crew so he can manage both responsibilities."

"Yes, I agreed that Raja, Connor, and I would meet with him." Ty's office door open and Felix stepped in. "I must go, there's much I need to attend to before the announcement. We'll see you tomorrow." With that Ty clicked off.

Jinx leaned back against the chair. In less than forty-eight hours everything for their kind was about to change. Tabitha was about to become Queen of the Tigers. There was bound to be backlash from it, and he had to be damn sure he'd have his house in order so the clan and his family were protected.

Jinx's Mate: Alaskan Tigers

Chapter Nineteen

The list of new Elder guards had been created—only one name left before they could end the discussion. Summer sat on the sofa with Claire playing at her feet, and Jinx next to her. Jackson sat across from them giving his input on the status of the potential guards.

"Let's discuss Meshell." She knew Jinx had been putting it off, and now it was time to confront it head on.

"You observed her training, what did you think?" Jackson inquired.

"I know next to nothing about hand-to-hand combat, weapons, or anything else that you covered with her today. She seemed good, and she's a good shot. But I think you need to tell me what you thought of her actions today." Summer tossed the question back at Jackson. Avery had never taught them any kind of combat skills, so even though Meshell looked good to her, it didn't mean she was.

"As I told Jinx before, Meshell is a good prospect. She takes orders well, and as you said she's a good shot. Even with as many hours as she puts in at the gym she's still outweighed and outpowered by most men. That could be an issue in a fight, if she can't shoot because innocents are in the way," Jackson explained.

"What happens when she's protecting my family and is overpowered?" Jinx asked.

"She's not going to be the only guard with them. When Meshell is on there will be three. We can have her assigned when I'm on duty if you'd prefer." Jackson leaned forward, resting his hands on his knees. "I've been training her on some tactical moves that will allow her to take down someone twice her size without using her gun. There's also the option of giving her a high powered stun gun, or a handgun that is armed with tranquilizers."

Jinx leaned forward, his gaze on Jackson. "You honestly believe she's up for the challenge and that Summer or Claire won't be in more danger while she's on watch?"

Jackson nodded. "With all due respect, I do. Giving her a chance will allow her to become a better guard, and she'll protect your family."

"Summer?" Jinx waited for her last words on the matter.

"I trust Jackson. If he believes she's ready, then she's ready."

"Very well." Jinx nodded. "She'll be the last guard, with the stipulation that she's only to be on duty when you or Carson are on and that she must continue her training. This will be a trial run, to make sure she's up for the duties which will be expected of her."

Seven guards for her and little Claire seemed like too many to Summer, especially since when she was safely in the house with Jinx she didn't need a guard. But Jinx wouldn't settle for anything less than six, and with Meshell as an add-on it left her with a total of seven. Jackson, Carson, Garth, Larry, Duncan, Hugo, and Meshell.

"If you'd like I can gather them and make the announcement. I know you have a lot to do before leaving in the morning," Jackson suggested.

Jinx nodded, lacing his fingers through Summer's. "That would be fine. I'm hoping to make it a quick trip to Alaska, there's much I need to deal with here, so not everyone will be going. Have Garth and Hugo prepare themselves. They will be the additional guards along with you and Carson."

Jackson stood. "Very well. I'll see to it."

"One last thing." Jinx grabbed the box sitting on the coffee table. "These are ear pieces, and I want all the guards to wear them. Lukas is handing them out to all the ground guards. Now that we've decided on Elder guards, they need to have them as well." He held it up so they could see it. "These are specifically designed for the Elder guards, and they have a second channel built in. By touching the red button on this side, the Elder team can hear any message delivered. If there's ever a breach of security, this will allow for us to communicate without everyone knowing what is happening. It stays in your ear at all times, and there's a sleep mode so it will only alert you if there's an emergency."

"Lukas mentioned the Alaskan Tigers having something similar. It will be great for the guards to know what's happening, and will allow us to keep everyone safe." Jackson took the box.

"If anyone has questions about them, Lukas will be available to assist," Jinx explained. "Unless something comes up, you're off duty once you've dealt with that. I'll be in this evening, Lukas will be coming up for a meeting, than we've got some work to do ourselves."

"I'll see you both in the morning then." Jackson took his exit.

"What did you have in mind for the evening?" Summer smirked, her fingers teasing over the back of his hand.

"My sweet lass, I'd love to take you to our bedroom and have my way with you until the sun comes up. Unfortunately, I have work I must attend to. With all my time in Alaska there were some things that fell to the wayside."

"I understand. Plus, there's always tonight." She glanced down at Claire, still silently playing with her dolls. "I should see if I can make any progress with her. She's having a good day, maybe a play date would be good for her."

"I'll see about arranging a play date with Lisa. She's nineteen months, but I think they might be a good fit. Lisa's shy and doesn't speak much. If it can be arranged there's a playroom that a lot of the children use, so that might be a good place. I'll have Carson take you there. I hope you understand."

"It's fine. Thank you. I'll get her ready."

He stopped her before she could stand. "Give me about twenty minutes to arrange it."

She nodded. "Sweetie, we're going to get ready and go for a play date. Would you like to meet a little girl about your age and play with her?"

Robin had told her to keep asking Claire questions as if she'd answer. It would provoke her, but not getting an answer every time was hard. What if Claire never spoke at all?

* * *

Papers where piled up in front of Jinx, each of them needing his attention. Attention he didn't have—he couldn't seem to focus. Summer and Claire had been gone over an hour at their play date.

Everything in him wanted to go to them, to see how things were going. The only thing that kept him rooted to his seat was he didn't want to disturb them if they were making progress. Claire's future mattered more to him than his curiosity. With a groan, he forced himself back to the paperwork.

"Jinx?" Lukas called.

He was so lost in his thoughts, he hadn't even heard the elevator. "In here." He pushed back his chair, thankful for the break.

"I saw Jackson on my way up, he's done with the guards. He's going to relieve Carson so he can pack and take over guard duties." Lukas sat down on the chair across from him. "The border is marked. Eric is nervous, but ready, so we'll be ready to go first thing in the morning. Any changes with Claire?"

"Not yet. She's still not speaking, but being here has seemed to relax her some. Hopefully going to Alaska won't disturb that."

"You could always leave them here and I can stay behind with them."

He shook his head. "Thank you, but no. We need to at least try with Robin. If she can't help, she may have some suggestions on what we can do."

"While we're on the subject of Claire...I really don't know how to say this."

"You don't feel the connection." He knew what Lukas was thinking.

"Yes. Why?"

"There's no blood relation between us, so we don't have the normal connection that is passed to the children of the clan members, and she's not old enough to commit to the clan. We're going to be blind to her for the next several years." Since Summer voiced her fears they'd been lurking in his mind. Claire was an unknown to them. Everything she witnessed might have sent her down a path she couldn't return from.

"What about Tex? Does he feel her? The connection from her parents should have passed down to him once he took over as Alpha, shouldn't it?"

"He's blind to her. Meaning one of two things, either the parents were never committed to Avery and he only had them under him because of force. Or..." Jinx couldn't bring himself to continue.

"Or she's already headed down a path we can't bring her back from. One where she'll become an enemy to us, and our kind." Lukas finished for him.

"Yes." The single word came out more like a whisper. "There's no way for us to tell until she starts showing signs."

"Then what?"

"Summer asked me the same thing last night." He leaned forward, gripping the pen in his hand until it shattered. "I'd have no choice. Summer believes I'd force her to leave the clan, but it's so much more than that."

"If she's a true enemy to us…"

He cut off Lukas before he could finish. "She'd have to be eliminated."

He had come to love the little lass, and thinking of what the future might bring terrified him and made him sick. Avery had done so much damage, but the one who might have suffered the most was Claire.

"I'm sorry."

"Me too. Claire deserves a chance, and we'll give it to her, but now that we know this it will always be in the back of our minds. We will always wonder if one day we'll wake up and she'd be against us." He dropped the destroyed pen in the trash bin and looked back at Lukas. "How do you stop something like that from happening? How do you get a child to put everything she witnessed behind her and embrace the good of our kind?"

"I don't have the answer. You know I'll do whatever I can to keep her from going down that path."

"It's more of an option for her because of everything she's seen. At that age, their brains are developing, they're impressionable. From the nightmares she's having I believe Avery tortured her mother while she watched. That could haunt a person for life." Part of him wished they had made Avery suffer as he made others suffer. But that would've only brought him and the others down to Avery's level; they were better than that.

"But now she's surrounded by love and a clan that cares. Don't give up hope, it's not too late." Lukas took a sip from the bottle of water he had. "Once we start giving up on her, then and only then is it too late for her."

"Giving up isn't an option, not until we know for sure it's too late."

How did one ever lose hope where their child was concerned? If the time came, he wondered if he would he be able to do his duty and take down Claire before she could hurt someone.

Chapter Twenty

It was midday in Alaska when they finally landed. For Summer and the rest of them, it was five hours later. They had much to do to get ready for Tabitha's announcement. By this time tomorrow, the whole world for tigers was going to change.

They'd have one Queen who ruled over all the Alphas. It also meant some major backlash was coming, and Tabitha, Ty, and their clan weren't the only targets. Tex and the Texas Tigers, Jinx and the West Virginia Tigers, and the Kodiak Bears all had to be on alert. They had to embrace a life where danger was around every corner, and any of them could die at any time.

"Summer," Robin called out, working her way toward them. "With everything that's going on I was thinking if I could get you and Claire right off the plane we could get it over with. That way Claire's not too tired. What do you think?"

"Sure." She nodded. Claire stood next to her holding her hand. "Jinx?"

"I need to speak with Ty, and the others. Can I catch up with you in a bit?"

"That's fine." Robin nodded. "We'll be in my cabin, just ask Adam or one of the others to direct you."

"Jackson goes with Summer," Jinx ordered. "I'll have Carson take your bags to our rooms and then he'll join you."

Robin led the way, quickly passing through the gathering crowd. "I'm sorry to catch you right when you landed, but if we can make some progress with Claire, I can work with her while you're here. We should take advantage of every moment we have for her sake."

"It's fine. I wanted to have this meeting today before things got busy with the announcement." Though she had hoped to spend a moment with Ben before being rushed off.

"Have there been any changes with Claire?"

She leaned down and picked Claire up, so they could keep up with Robin as they made their way to the cabin. "She's not talking, but she's adjusting well. We had a wonderful play date yesterday with another little girl, Lisa."

"That's great." Robin opened the cabin door. "How is she adjusting to the guards?"

"She's doing well with Jackson." She walked in, and sat Claire next to the fire with her stuffed tiger. "And she's doing well with Carson and Garth. Larry, he's in Texas at the moment, but he looks a little too much like Avery and that seems to be scaring her. As for the rest, she hasn't met them really. Well, she saw Hugo on the plane but she didn't actually meet him."

"Have you thought about assigning Larry somewhere else then?"

"He's a good guard, and one that needs to be on the team to keep the Alpha Female and Claire safe." Jackson answered before Summer could.

"Very well. I was only considering Claire."

"So are we." Jackson stepped closer to Claire, in a protective gesture. "As Captain of the Guards, Summer and Claire are my top priorities. Larry is part of the team but we'll make sure he keeps his distance until Claire has a chance to warm up to him. Sheltering her from him will only let the fear continue. He's a good man and will protect her, she'll see that."

"Fine then, if you'll both give me a few minutes alone with Claire, I'll see what I can do."

"Actually, Jinx and I discussed this…Jackson can wait by the door out of eyesight, but I won't leave her," Summer said. "Anytime she's along without Jackson, Jinx, or myself, it seems to set things back further. She's come to trust us, and leaving her now in a new place could prove to be disastrous."

Robin took a seat by the fireplace. "That's not how I prefer to work, but as you are the Alpha Female I'll let it slide *this time*. In the future I'll need to do this alone in order to make progress with her. I would ask that you step out of direct eyesight as well."

She gave a nod to Jackson who reluctantly took a place by the door. Then, with a reminder to herself they were doing this to help Claire, she stepped back. As soon as she stepped away Claire pulled her legs up against her chest, hugging the stuffed tiger to her.

"Claire, my name's Robin and I'm here to help you." She slipped forward on her chair, bringing herself closer to Claire.

Summer's heart broke as she watched Claire begin to rock herself. The fear was clear in her body as she made herself as small as she could get. Even Jackson had taken a step forward.

"Can you tell me what happened to you in the cellar? What happened to your mother?"

With every question Robin asked, tears flowed quicker down Claire's face, her body trembling with sobs. Summer wasn't sure how much more she could take. Her body screamed to go to her little girl, that this wasn't right. Everything that seemed to be happening seemed to push Claire further back.

The door flew open, nearly hitting Jackson, and in walked Jinx. "Enough." His voice echoed with authority as he closed the distance to Claire. "It's okay, lass." He picked her up, wrapping his arms around her and holding her tight to his chest.

Robin shot to her feet. "What is the meaning of this? You asked for my help."

"Consider it retracted then." He ran his hand over Claire's back. "I might not be able to feel her emotions but I can tell you for damn sure you're not helping her."

"I have to find a way to break through. Bringing up those bad memories might help her talk. I don't have time to pussyfoot around it, you're only here for two days!"

"All you're doing is terrifying her. I was watching from the window and I could see her retreating further into herself. We haven't made a lot of progress yet, but what we have is better than nothing. I won't have you scaring her back to the terrified little lass we found in Texas." He turned and stalked toward the door. "Come along, Summer, we're done here."

She went to him, with Jackson taking up the rear.

"I thought you had other things to deal with?" Summer asked, coming down the steps to where Carson and Garth waited.

"I decided my family was more important and that I should be there in case Claire said anything." He rubbed Claire's back, trying to ease the sobs. "I'm sorry. I shouldn't have left you alone."

"I wasn't alone, Jackson was there." She slid under his arm, pressing herself to him and gently laying a hand on Claire. "I couldn't stand what was happening but I kept telling myself if it helped it was going to be worth it."

"She has no experience with children or anyone who is mute from terror." He held her for a moment before continuing. "You said it yourself, she was making progress yesterday with the play date, so we'll do things our way. Research what we need and if it doesn't work we'll find someone who specializes in this. I won't have someone terrifying her."

"We should move along," Jackson suggested. "She's standing in the window watching us."

"Come on, lass, let's get you and Claire settled into our cabin. Then I have to get back to work." He brushed his lips against Claire's forehead. "Little lass, how would you like it if Jackson read you a story?" She nodded her head against his shoulder without looking up.

"Then that's what we'll do." Summer ran a hand through Claire's hair, pulling it away from her face. "I'm sorry, sweetie. Things are going to be okay. Daddy and I will make sure of it."

* * *

With his family secure in the cabin, Jinx made his way across the compound back to see the progress and to check with Lukas on what he had missed. Seeing that fear in Claire had pushed him over the edge; his tiger was ready to spring forth and attack. This was more than being an Alpha. This was parenthood. The love for a child could make a person do things they would never do to protect that child.

"Jinx."

He turned to see Adam strolling toward him. "Everything okay? You look worried."

"I was just by the cabin to see Robin. She's upset."

"What do you want me to say?" As the wind picked up, he adjusted his cowboy hat. "I can't apologize. With someone in Claire's condition and her age, she took it too far."

"Actually, it was me who came to apologize. Robin is so eager to help. She went at it straight forward, and with a child that young she shouldn't have." Adam held out a stack of papers. "This is all the research we gathered. Maybe something in it will help Claire."

"Thank you." He took the papers, and told himself he'd look over it as soon as things were over in Alaska. "Robin is a good thing for our people. Especially those in the Ohio and Texas clans who have been abused. I saw the progress she made with Harmony and

Tex with the abuse they suffered. I just don't think her specialty is children."

"I understand you probably won't want it, but if you ever need it, Robin is still here to help. Though it might be best if it isn't until Claire is speaking. I can give you my word there won't be a repeat of what happened today. She does feel extremely guilty."

"I'll keep that in mind." He wanted to tell Adam it wasn't a big deal, but it was. "We all make mistakes. If Claire doesn't have any lasting issues, and this hasn't set her back further, then no damage done. Now I must find Lukas."

"He's with Ty and that kid Eric, they're in the Nerd Crew room with Connor."

"Perfect." Jinx headed that way, hoping that for Lukas's sake Eric was living up to what Ty needed from him.

Across the grounds everyone seemed to be moving at an escalated pace, getting things prepared for tomorrow. The Alaskan Tigers knew Tabitha's destiny, but the rest of the tiger population was about to find out. Everyone was checking the perimeter, making sure the fence and cameras were all in place. Preparing themselves if there was an attack.

Tomorrow the announcement would go out, with Jinx, Lukas, Tex, and Ben at Ty and Tabitha's side supporting them. Devon, Taber, and Thorben would be there representing the Kodiak Bears. It would be a joint affair showing their support for the union. Directly after the announcement, Jinx and his crew would head back to West

Virginia, Tex to Texas, and Devon back to the Brown's Island in Nome. Everyone wanted to be home in case of an uproar.

Tomorrow's the day we've been all waiting for...

Chapter Twenty-One

The team gathered in the ballroom, one final run down of what was about to happen before they'd take their places. Jinx stood with his arms around Summer, while Claire played happily at their feet, anxious to get things going. Lukas had the equipment set up, ready to be activated.

"The clans that aren't available at this time, or don't have computers, how will they get the message?" Tex inquired.

"Anyone who doesn't log in within thirty minutes to watch the announcement, the system will call and deliver it through the phones. That should cover everyone," Lukas explained, as Eric fixed the lights.

"If not, we'll have to figure something out for any clan that doesn't have the news within the next few hours." Ty stood next to the platform, Tabitha looking a little pale at his side.

"Are we ready then?" Jinx ran his fingers down Summer's body. He was anxious to get this over with and get back home. This wasn't just a new beginning for all the tigers; he was on the path of a new beginning for himself, one that he wanted in West Virginia. He found it amazing that mating changed so much, making him leave his traveling days behind to settle down, giving his family stability.

"Why doesn't everyone get into position? I need a moment with Tabitha." Ty led Tabitha to the side, his arm around her shoulders.

"Jackson!" Jinx called out.

Summer raised an eyebrow at him. "We don't need a guard. You're going to be right there."

"You never know what could happen, so stay with Jackson. Carson is just outside if he's needed."

"I'm right here as well." Ben came up to stand next to them. "Sorry I haven't had much time to see you."

"It's been a whirlwind of a trip, and thankfully almost over. I never realized how much I preferred the quiet life until now." She stepped out of Jinx's embrace and hugged her brother. "It's still good to see you."

"I spoke with Tex. As soon as things calm down, I'm going to slip away for a few days and come visit you. I thought it would be better for Claire, and Jinx approved." He squatted down in front of Claire. "Did you miss your Uncle Ben?"

Surprising them all, Claire leaned forward and wrapped her little arms around Ben's neck, the stuffed tiger he'd given her still clutched in her hand.

"I think she missed you," Summer confirmed.

"I got to go." Jinx nodded to everyone already in their places. "Remember to stay back, I don't want you and Claire in any more danger." He kissed her and then leaned down and kissed Claire on the top of her head. "I want you to stay with Mommy, Uncle Ben, and Jackson."

Stepping onto the platform, he took his position, which would be next to Ty when he joined them. Raja was on the other side of Tabitha with Devon next to him, while Taber, Thorben, and Tex stood behind them. Solidarity.

He reminded himself why they were doing it. It wasn't so there was one ruler, it was for their future, one that would make them free. It was for his family, for Summer and Claire, and all the other shifters. No longer would they have to hide. All over the country tiger shifters were dying out; this was going to bring life back to their people.

If Tabitha produced an heir their numbers would explode. If she failed, or their enemies were able to kill her or Ty, they would slowly die out, and tiger shifters would fade until there was nothing left. That sent Jinx's thoughts spiraling downward with a glance at his family as he thought about the one thing that had compelled him to dedicate himself to Tabitha. *The legend.*

No one was sure if they'd be able to continue their line, and would simply fade out with time, or if they would just die with her. Either way it would mean the end of their species.

Even though it made no sense to Jinx, the rogues were desperate to kill her. Pierce had drilled into them that she was an enemy, and that she wanted them to band together so she could kill them all. As insane as it all sounded, some bought into it. Now this announcement would bring more danger to her and everyone surrounding her.

"Okay, we're ready." Ty nodded to Lukas as they stepped into their places. Tabitha looked better than she had, the color back in her cheeks. Whatever Ty had said to her worked. Felix and Adam took their places on the ends, their weapons visible.

Lukas nodded, letting them know they were on.

"Hello, Alphas of the United States clans. I'm Tabitha. My mate Ty and I have an announcement that concerns everyone." She paused, squared her shoulders, and began. "The legend of a tiger coming to unite all of us as one, bringing peace among all, and one day announcing our species to the world is true. I am that one, the tigress here to save our kind. This is the official announcement that I've claimed my destiny and my title as Queen of the Tigers."

Ty placed his hand on her back. "If you're not with us, you're against us. Any enemy who makes a move on us or our allies will be dealt with severely. As you can see we are surrounded by people who stand together for our cause." Ty paused and glanced toward his Lieutenant. "Raja, the Alaskan Tigers' Lieutenant." Raja nodded.

"Jinx from the West Virginia Tigers." Jinx stepped forward, and when he stepped back Ty continued. "Tex, the new Alpha of the Texas Tigers." Since Tex was behind Jinx he couldn't step forward so he raised his hand instead. "Devon of the Kodiak Bears and two of his sons, Taber and Thorben."

"The two at the end are members of my Elder guards. Felix, the Captain of my Guards." Tabitha paused as Felix stepped forward, looking menacing. "Adam, his second."

"Korbin of the Ohio Tigers, who couldn't make it today, is also an ally," Ty said. "There are many more who aren't pictured, both in this clan and among our allies. So before you decide you're against us, consider what you're up against." Ty glanced at his mate. "If you're with us, you'll see a world you never have before. One that allows us to live without hiding ourselves, or risk being experimented on. It won't happen overnight, but this is one step toward it."

Tabitha cleared her throat. "We ask that if you wish to join us in making a better world for our species that you get in touch with us. At the bottom of the screen you'll see a phone number and email that you can contact us at. If we don't hear from you within forty-eight hours we'll assume you are against us." Tabitha paused as Lukas got the information on screen. "This is the first step toward a brighter world for all of us. Don't delay, as there's much to do."

Lukas ended the transmission, sending it out for all the tiger clans to see, and sending it as a file to be downloaded for anyone who wasn't online.

It all seemed anticlimactic. With nothing else to do Jinx stepped away and went to his family. "Now we wait. Hopefully within the next forty-eight hours we have everyone on board."

"Otherwise we could have a war on our hands." Adam leaned against one of the tables.

Ty shook his head. "I think it's clear the war is already on our hands and is just beginning."

"Dealing with the Ohio and Texas clans was just the beginning of what is about to come." Raja slipped his hand into Bethany's. "We all have to be ready because the future is going to be a bloody thing."

"From everything I heard, this was the right decision, so we shouldn't doubt it now." Summer leaned her head against Jinx's chest.

"Not doubting, just concerned." Tabitha shook her head. "We'll need to be cautious of everything and everyone now."

"Let's sit down before everyone starts rushing off." Ty pulled out a seat for Tabitha. "We're going to need to be cautious of every Alpha, even once they commit to our goal. Unlike with the clan right now there's no way to determine if they are truly with us. We will only have their word. Until they prove themselves we need to be on guard."

Tabitha laid her hand over Ty's. "We didn't mention the book that was handed down through the generations of my family, and has been leading me on this journey, because we can't risk it falling into the wrong hands. Only the ones gathered in this room, and my guards, know about it. If it were to get out the danger would be even greater."

"We have the longest journey ahead of us, so we should be going." Jinx lifted Claire into his arms. "You know how to reach us when you need us."

Ty stepped forward and offered his hand. "Thank you for everything. We'll see you again soon."

He shook his hand, before nodding to Jackson. "I hope it is on good terms and not in the midst of a battle."

"Eric and I will be out in a minute," Lukas hollered packing up his equipment.

Jackson opened the door, and stepped into the hall before allowing Jinx to lead his family out.

"Come on, lass, let's get you home."

"I don't know what I was expecting when we came, but I guess I thought more would happen, I suppose."

"Me too, lass, but I have a feeling we're going to have all the excitement we could want in the coming months."

"You think it's going to be bad?"

They stepped outside, heading to the plane. Garth and Hugo were waiting at the bottom of the stairs. Once Lukas and Eric were done they'd be on their way back home.

"There's no real way to tell, but I do suspect there's going to be more Alphas like Avery in the mix, and others who are just resistant to the change," Jinx said. "The idea of having Tabitha overseeing everything is going to make others nervous."

"It doesn't make you nervous?"

"No, not really. I know Tabitha and Ty are trying to take over. They want to make things better for everyone, and make sure there're no more Alphas like Avery." He paused at the bottom of the steps, letting the cold air blow around him.

"Do you really think one day we won't be able to hide what we are?"

He nodded. "Someday we won't have to worry about others finding out and trying to experiment on us. It's going to take some time. We need to get everyone together, and eliminate any problems before we go public."

There was still a lot to be done before that, rules that had to be established, and issues that had to be eliminated. Most of all, they had to do away with the rogues who were eager to kill Tabitha.

Epilogue

The forty-eight hours were almost up and less than half of the clans were on board with Tabitha. Many of the others had questions about what everything entailed, giving Tabitha and Ty a lot to handle. A handful had flat out refused to have Tabitha or anyone else above them. Jinx glanced at the list and noticed there were still five clans they hadn't heard from, one way or the other.

The Minnesota Alpha, Calvin, was demanding an audience and insisting his questions were answered before he would make any commitment. There was something more to it. Did Calvin plan to demand something in return for his loyalty?

"You're not going to work all night again, are you?"

Jinx glanced up to find Summer standing in the doorway, in a cute emerald green baby doll nighty. "Umm, not if you're going to wear that, lass."

"Wear? I was thinking you'd take it off me."

"I think we can arrange that." He scooted his chair back from the desk. "Come here."

"Hmm, another office christening." She sashayed to him. "You've been working too hard, too much on your mind. Let me reduce your stress."

"Everything has changed. I'm just adjusting to it, and trying to protect my family and our clan."

"I know, love. Did Ty mention if he'd approved Eric working with the Nerd Crew?" She slipped into his lap, running her fingers up his chest.

"Yes, that's all set. Which will allow for Lukas to have less to deal with."

"Good. Then you can give him more responsibilities and spend more time with us." She leaned in, pressing her lips to his neck. "Now come to bed and take this off me."

"That's the perfect way to end a long day." He slipped his arm under her and stood. As he carried her to the bedroom, screams erupted from Claire's room. "I guess that puts any plans on hold." He set her down.

"It won't always be like this. Each day there's progress, especially when she's with little Lisa," Summer told him as they raced to Claire.

He flung opened the door and their little lass sat in the middle of the bed, clutching the stuffed tiger that had become her source of security.

"Lass, we're here."

Summer went to her and picked her up. "It's okay, sweetie. It was only a bad dream, we're here."

"Mommy." Claire cried and held onto Summer's neck.

"Did she?" He stepped into the room, a lump forming in his throat. Did he really just hear their little girl speak?

"She did." Summer pulled Claire back so she could look at her. "Sweetie, say it again."

"Mommy." This time the word came out timid.

"Oh, my little lass." He went to them, wrapping his arms around both of them. "I'm so proud of you."

"Daddy." She reached toward him.

With those two simple words everything fell together. He went from being a bachelor who wasn't really looking for a mate, to a family man. Claire might not have been his flesh and blood but she was his daughter. Hearing her speak gave him hope it wasn't too late to save her from the darkness.

Whatever happened in the coming months with Tabitha taking over as Queen of the Tigers, he'd help as much as he could—but his priorities had changed. He had a family, and they were his responsibly above all else.

Jinx's Mate: Alaskan Tigers

Preview: A Touch of Death

The death of Jael James' mother meant it was time to face her destiny as the Grim Reaper. Her first spirit shows up after being murdered, demanding the killer be caught before she can cross over. If a serial killer on the loose wasn't bad enough, it turned out to be a demon sent by Lucifer to test her.

Death is there to guide her as she makes the journey into the unknown, but he seems to have his own agenda—which involves getting her naked. He wants to show her what they could have together. But then there's Nathan, who wants to be more than just her paramedic partner. Competing with Death for her attention might be more than Nathan can handle.

Will Jael find a balance that will keep her secret safe, or will her new role as Grim Reaper force her to walk away from the two most important men in her life?

Jinx's Mate: Alaskan Tigers

Prologue

Tears welled in Jael's eyes as she sat at her dying mother's bedside. As an adult it wasn't supposed to be this devastating to lose a parent. No longer would her mother suffer. She wouldn't have to put up with harsh criticism for talking to *people* no one else could see.

Jael rested her head against the back of the chair, the rough wood digging into her skull. The feeling grounded her, helped her force the tears back. Time with her mother was nearing its end, and she didn't want to waste it by crying. Opening her eyes, she saw a man leaning against the wall. Dressed in black, his jeans and T-shirt clung tight. His clothing was a dark contrast to his creamy white skin and the bright white wall behind him. His hair fell just above his ears, reminding her of spilled ink, a few stray pieces dangling just above his sapphire eyes that sparkled with hints of silver.

Drop dead gorgeous is an understatement. This was no time to let her hormones get out of control. Her mother needed her to remain focused.

"Can I help you?" She raised an eyebrow at him. There was no way he was medical staff. He continued to lean against the wall, completely ignoring her. Her unease rose, but instead of giving into it she pushed back from her chair and stood. "This is a private room and visiting hours are over. Please leave."

"I'm here to see her." He nodded toward her mother.

"She's not up for visitors now. If you could come back tomorrow maybe she'll be ready then." In no mood to deal with him, she reached to the side of the bed, her finger hovering just above the nurse call button.

"Ann." His voice floated through the room, with a hint of mystery.

She eyed him with anger for his lack of respect for her privacy. "I don't know how you know my mother, but I asked you to leave. Go or I'll call security."

A light chuckle teased the air. "I wouldn't recommend that."

"What's that supposed to mean?" she snapped.

"Jael?" Ann's eyes were glazed from the drugs that coursed through her body.

As if summoned by her mother's voice, the man moved away from the wall and came toward the bed. "Ann, it's time to tell her."

"No, not yet." Tears welled in Ann's eyes, as she tugged the breathing mask away from her face. "I need more time."

"I've given you as much time as I could, but it's nearly up. Don't make me deliver the news." With that he disappeared as quickly as he'd appeared. He just vanished. Jael startled, jumping back, then sinking into her chair, shocked and near panic.

"What the hell just happened?" She pinched herself to make sure it wasn't all a dream. She'd had so little sleep the last few days, she wouldn't have been surprised if she had dozed off or hallucinated the whole thing.

"Destiny has been revealed." Ann's breathy voice cut through Jael's thoughts.

"What?"

"I'm dying." When Jael started to interrupt, Ann shook her head to stop her. "Don't, just hear me out. It's going to sound bizarre so I need to say it *all* before you interrupt. All these years, people thought I was crazy, seeing people they don't. It's because I'm the Grim Reaper."

"The what?" Jael had been asked to keep quiet, but her heart was slamming against her chest, and she couldn't stop herself. "Mom, I think it's the drugs the doctor gave you. Please rest."

"It's not the drugs. If you trace our family history back, you'll see that the first female born in each generation has been given the ability to see the dead. We are the Grim Reaper. Without us, the spirits stuck in limbo cannot cross over into the light. It's our calling, our destiny. He will help you along your path, assist you with what you need." She gripped Jael's hand, taking a moment to catch her breath. "I've sheltered you while I could, but now that my time on this Earth is coming to an end, it's time for you to take my place."

She heard her mother's words but couldn't believe them. It had to be the medication that was making her delusional. Her mom had always been eccentric, talking to people no one else could see. But a Grim Reaper? They didn't exist. When you died, there was no limbo, just Heaven or Hell, your body turning to dust in the ground, nothing more.

"Mom, just rest."

After years of being a paramedic in Crystal Falls, Montana, she had seen death more times than she cared to remember, and never once had a ghost risen out of a body asking for help. It just didn't happen. When someone died, there was nothing left for them in this world. Even if there was life after death, there was no room in Jael's life to help those who'd passed on. Death was already an unavoidable part of her job, but to see the spirits of those she couldn't save sounded like more than she could handle.

Why worry? I don't believe what she's saying anyway.

"You need to understand what will happen. Things will change for you when I die."

Jael squeeze her mother's hand. "It will be fine. There are always changes in life. Don't worry, I'll be fine. I'll miss you, but you'll be with Dad again. Everything is going to be fine."

"Your father…" Ann's smile was warm and wishful, as she reached her hand out to touch the length of something, but all Jael could see was thin air. "He's always been with me, but to actually touch him again will make up for leaving you. I've always wanted to protect you, Jael. I love you."

"I know, Mom. I love you too. Sleep, I'll figure everything out, it's going to be fine."

The drugs helping to lessen Ann's pain from the bone cancer were pulling her under again, sleep's long fingers reaching out to her to drag her under. In the back of Jael's mind, she wondered if this would be the last time her mother ever spoke to her. Ann had already lived two weeks past the doctor's expectation.

Unable to sit, she paced the room, her mind running in circles. She needed fresh air and wished she could open a window. With little choice she strolled into the bathroom, grabbed a paper towel, wet it, and placed it over her forehead. The coolness against her warm skin refreshed her. Now she hoped to find some strong, hot coffee to help get her through the night.

"Your mother told you what you are." Death leaned against the doorframe between her mother's room and the bathroom. His arms were crossed over his chest as he watched her. "I can unleash your powers and allow you to see across the planes to the land of the dead…if you're ready."

She threw the towel in the trash and brushed past him. "I'll never be ready. I don't want that life, find someone else."

"So you believe Ann, then?" The corner of his mouth tugged up in a smirk.

"Hell no! I mean…I don't know." She dragged her hand through her long blonde hair, unable to look at him. "Mom's was always been a little eccentric. If she truly believes she sees people others don't, then whatever, but I don't want to be a part of it. I don't want her life."

"It's your legacy. There is only one Grim Reaper at a time, and you're it. You will carry on the line when your mother passes, as your child will, and their child."

Spinning around, she glared at him. "Legacy? Why didn't she tell me about it before? How did she expect me to handle or believe it when it's dropped on me like this?"

"I didn't agree with Ann keeping this from you. You should have been told so you could have adjusted to it. As you aged she should have allowed me to unleash your powers slowly, giving you time to process everything and learn from her. Now you'll only have time for a crash course before you step into her place."

"I don't want this. To be seen as crazy as she was is no life. I have everything I want, a good job, a beautiful condo. Just leave me alone." She sank into the chair next to the hospital bed, tears streaming down her face.

"If I could give you that I would, but it's your legacy. You have no choice but to step into her place once she passes. I will return."

With the slightest breeze against the back of her neck, she knew he was gone. "I'd rather take your place, Mom, than live with this curse."

Marissa Dobson

Born and raised in the Pittsburgh, Pennsylvania area, Marissa Dobson now resides about an hour from Washington, D.C. She's a lady who likes to keep busy, and is always busy doing something. With two different college degrees, she believes you're never done learning.

Being the first daughter to an avid reader, this gave her the advantage of learning to read at a young age. Since learning to read she has always had her nose in a book. It wasn't until she was a teenager that she started writing down the stories she came up with.

Marissa is blessed with a wonderful supportive husband, Thomas. He's her other half and allows her to stay home and pursue her writing. He puts up with all her quirks and listens to her brainstorm in the middle of the night.

Her writing buddies Max (a cocker spaniel) and Dawne (a beagle mix) are always around to listen to her bounce ideas off them. They might not be able to answer, but they are helpful in their own ways.

She love to hear from readers so send her an email at marissa@marissadobson.com or visit her online at http://www.marissadobson.com.

Jinx's Mate: Alaskan Tigers

Other Books by Marissa Dobson

Tiger Time

The Tiger's Heart

Tigress for Two

Night with a Tiger

Trusting a Tiger

Jinx's Mate

Snowy Fate

Sarah's Fate

Mason's Fate

As Fate Would Have It

A Touch of Death

Learning to Live

Learning What Love Is

Her Cowboy's Heart

Half Moon Harbor Resort Volume One

Restoring Love

Winterbloom

Unexpected Forever

Losing to Win

Christmas Countdown

The Surrogate

Clearwater Romance Volume One

Secret Valentine

The Twelve Seductive Days of Christmas

Praise:

Alaskan Tigers

Tiger Time:

This is the first book that I have read from Marissa Dobson and it definitely won't be my last. I loved the tiger shapeshifter aspect of this book which I haven't read much about in previous books. ~ Jennifer at Books-n-Kisses

When I first read a review for Tiger Time, I knew this was a must read. Now I know that it is definitely a must read for anyone that like were romances. It's definitely one of those that draws you immediately into the story, and never lets you go... a wonderfully written story of a woman's journey into the unknown and a man who would show her to her destiny. LOVED IT!!!! Looking forward to the next one in the series. ~ Addicted to Romance

The Tiger's Heart:

This book was so interesting and I loved it. Steamy with lots of twists and turns. Recommend this to anyone who likes Shifter type books. ~ Amazon Reader

Tigress for Two:

And the plot thickens. I am really enjoying how the overall story arc of this series is going. There are so many players that it is fascinating to watch the plot unfold. Everyone's story is connected, but not in the ways that I had originally anticipated and that makes it all the more fun to read. ~ Delphina Reads too Much

Wow, Tigress for Two was everything I'd hoped it would be after reading some of Marissa Dobson's other books. She packed a whollop, enticing the reader with angst, suspense, romance and suspense...oh did I say that twice? Well good cause I meant to, because she did a great job of keeping the reader in suspense throughout the whole story. I never knew what was coming next but i was so intrigued I couldn't put the book down. I seriously never imagined mixing shifter species but it was done well. ~ A Passion for Romance

Stormkin Series

Storm Queen:

To use the word amazing is not too strong when describing this book. I've never read anything like it and I loved every minute of it. Do yourself a favor of buying this book, if you don't you'll be missing out. ~Rebecca Royce, bestselling author of the The Westervelt Wolves.

This was a great new addition to the paranormal romance world, it almost had a Urban Fantasy feel because the sex wasn't the main focus of the story and I LOVED that! I thought each scene was done

so well! I will be continuing this series! I can't wait for the next one!
~ Amazon Reader

Clearwater Series
Winterblom:

I found Winterbloom to be a sweet and delightful little romance. Ms. Dobson does a wonderful job of creating visual scenes that allow the reader to feel as though they are right there within the story. ~ Romancing the Book

Unexpected Forever:

Unexpected Forever made me cry. I'll admit it; I teared up quite a few times actually...Marissa has yet again written an amazing story full of emotions and detail. I totally recommend reading Unexpected Forever and other great works by Marissa. ~ Crystal Out There

Fate Series
As Fate Would Have It:

This book has all 3 of the Fate Stories in it! Each are about mountain lion shifters and finding their mates! All are sweet, Heartwarming, Romantic stories! I can't wait to read more by Marissa Dobson! ~Amazon Reader

Snowy Fate:

This was a very quick read, but with just a few pages, Marissa Dobson is able to get to the heart of this story. ~ Cocktails & Books

I really enjoyed Snowy Fate. I hope that you take the time to learn that no matter how hard you try you can't fight fate. ~ Books-n-Kisses

I thought this one was just perfect in length. There was enough background that I felt I knew the characters well and their attraction was believable. Fate has a way of making a HEA very real. I definitely recommend this one! ~ From the TBR Pile

CPSIA information can be obtained at www.ICGtesting.com
Printed in the USA
LVOW11s0207210614

391009LV00001B/277/P